DESERT BOUND

Caine's Liberation Series: Book One

Ren Stinnett

Edge House Publishing

Edge House Publishing
Riverside, CA
www.edgehousepublishing.com

Cover design by Larry Frazier
Desert Bound/Ren Stinnett – 1st ed. 2024
Printed in the United States of America

This book is dedicated to Sir John and Ken, my real-life Liam and Rik. These amazing men have supported me in ways they may not even realize. I am forever in debt for their compassion, wisdom, guidance, and love of all things kink.

"I have been a hundred times at a loss to know why we should be ashamed to speak of what Nature was not ashamed to create."

PIETRO ARTINO

CHAPTER ONE

I adjust my dick, strangely turned on by the ridiculous scene playing out in front of me. My boyfriend is fixated on believing our married buddy wants to hook up with us, and he's trying to prove his point tonight. We met Jon and his wife, Karyn, last year at Atomic Fitness in Albuquerque during a group interval class. The class was shit, but Glenn and I still lift there with Jon three nights a week. I told Glenn he is crazy, but he's determined to prove his point. Glenn can be headstrong, to say the least: it's a cop thing.

Jon's wife is out of town this weekend, so Glenn invited him to our place to watch the Diamondbacks/Angels game. Glenn's plan is simple: get Jon drunk enough to want to have sex with us. I don't think that's how it works in the real world, but Glenn seems obsessed with the idea that Jon is secretly gay and waiting for us to activate his hidden power. Part of me feels I should be offended my boyfriend wants to have sex with someone else, but I'm just drunk enough to be intrigued. I'm twenty-six years old and have only had sex with two people: Glenn and that random girl in high school. Maybe I'm due for a little adventure.

I met Glenn in high school back when we were on the wrestling team, but we didn't start dating until after I graduated from nursing school. I was twenty-one by then and Glenn was already a police officer. The first few years were awkward because Glenn didn't want his coworkers knowing he was gay. We're not closeted, technically, but Glenn prefers we remain discreet about our relationship. He mellowed, somewhat, after we moved into this apartment together. Jon and Karyn know we're gay, as do both of our parents.

Jon's sitting on the floor in front of the sofa with his head against Glenn's knee. Glenn smiles at me, pointing at Jon's head.

He's crazy.

The three of us have already burned through a case of beer and have progressed to tequila shots by the eighth inning. The game is tight, but I'm more interested in watching the real game: Glenn pretending not to flirt with Jon.

The Diamondbacks win and Glenn pretends to be excited even though he has little interest in baseball. He and Jon drink another shot to celebrate, then Glenn begins rubbing Jon's shoulders. Jon doesn't seem to mind, which is interesting. I'm guessing my gaydar may be broken because I've never seen a hint of Jon wanting anything from us other than friendship, but Glenn is a cop and insists he can read people better than I. We have never come close to messing around with anyone else during our relationship and I don't know where all this energy is coming from, but he hasn't stopped talking about getting Jon naked for the past few months.

Glenn winks at me. I just shake my head because he's the drunkest I've seen in years.

They turn to Xbox and play Call of Duty.

Glenn could be right and I may be oblivious, but I'm too buzzed to take this seriously. There's no denying Jon is attractive, though. He's tall and lean like a runner, with reddish-brown hair and ridiculously blue eyes. He has a big dick from what I can tell through his gym shorts. We don't have many male friends, because Glenn has never introduced me to his cop buddies and the nurses at my hospital are mostly women. I don't want to fuck up our friendship with Jon.

"Caine," Jon says to me as he taps my leg. He points over his shoulder to Glenn, who is passed out on the sofa.

"I didn't even see that happen."

Jon shrugs. "Want to play a few rounds?"

I nod and watch Jon's ass as he walks down the hall to the bathroom. He comes back, pours us each a shot, and plops down on the floor in front of me. I'm not as good at the game and become frustrated after a few rounds. It's nearly eleven-thirty and I'm ready to hit the sheets even though I don't work tomorrow.

Glenn is snoring, so I stand and down my shot. "I'm off to bed, man."

"Mind if I crash here tonight?"

"Of course not; the guest room is all yours." Jon asks if he can use the shower, so I show him where we keep the towels. I try to wake Glenn but he's out hard like nobody's business. I pull a blanket out from the cabinet and try to make him comfortable, as the nights are still pretty cold here in March.

Jon is in the main bathroom, so I use the half-bath to pee and wash my face. I hesitate as I walk to our bedroom, imagining how nice it would be to watch Jon showering. I'm crazy-tempted to open the bathroom door, but I shrug it off and continue into the bedroom. Stripping down to my underwear, I turn off the lights and crawl into bed. A thought of Glenn sneaking into the shower with Jon makes me hard and I start jacking off, picturing Glenn sliding his fat cock in Jon's ass. Maybe Jon prefers being the aggressor? I lick the palm of my hand and rub saliva down my shaft, slowly pulling down and back until my balls ache.

I jump at the sound of the shower stopping and pull my hand from my dick.

Jon's humming a familiar tune, then I hear him bump into something and curse. I feel Jon walk into the dark bedroom a few minutes later. His silhouette hovers above me at the side of the bed.

I wonder if he knows I'm awake.

A minute or so passes before he walks around the bed and lifts the covers, sliding into bed so close I can feel the heat of the shower radiating from his skin.

"Such a tease," I whisper.

"Nope," is his only response as he pushes further against me.

Seriously?

I turn on my side, facing Jon's back. I run my fingers down his exposed arm, so lightly I barely make contact with his warm skin. I'm nervous, and prepared for him to pull away. Instead, he rolls over and pushes me on my back with a soft laugh. He fumbles with the sheets and climbs up so that he is straddling me. I didn't even sense a change in energy, but it's as if my touching his arm flipped some switch. He leans down and kisses me, hard and clumsy.

I don't know what the fuck is going on. I want to yell for Glenn to join us but fear anything I do will pull Jon back into reality. I reach for his neck, unable to see anything but his silhouette, and guide his mouth to mine in an attempt to control the kissing before he breaks one of my teeth. He chews my lips and neck for several minutes while making a terrible attempt to pull the sheets out from between us. I help him with the sheets and massage his tight chest as he continues kissing me. He tastes of tequila and corn chips.

My cock throbs so hard it draws his attention. "You have a huge cock."

This is so stupid-awkward and I don't know what to say aside from "thanks".

"Can I touch it?

I nod before realizing he probably can't see me, so I respond by pulling my boxer briefs down.

Jon fumbles around with a pillow and slides down until I feel his breath on my hard dick. This is insane. He licks the tip a few times, rubbing my abs.

"Fucking-A," he laughs. I hear him inhale, then he wraps his lips around the head and works his way down the shaft. He's clumsy, too fast, and keeps gagging every time he tries to deep-throat me. I have to give him credit for trying but suspect he has very little, if any, experience sucking dick. I grab his hair and force him to slow down, guiding him through the motion. His mouth is tight, so different from Glenn's.

"There you go," I whisper. My voice sounds foreign, as if I have become another person. "Just like that, buddy. No rush."

Jon mumbles something around my dick that sound appreciative. I rub his shoulders, forcing myself not to grab the back of his head and force my dick down his throat. He keeps at it for a few minutes and, hot as this may be, his stubble is tearing me apart.

"Let's try something else," I say as I roll him over on his back. Pinning him down with my weight, I lick his smooth chest. This elicits a happy groan from him. I take my time, having fun working my way down his torso until my face is hovering over his cock. I wish I can see it and am tempted to turn on the lights, but I don't want to break this spell. Tracing my tongue from the tip of his dick down to his hairy balls makes him freeze in silence. All I hear is Jon's light panting and Glenn's snoring.

Jon groans as I wrap my hand around his balls and swallow his dick. His dick is slimmer than Glenn's, but longer. I tease and edge him slowly for a good twenty minutes until he is gasping and begging me to stop.

"You're gonna make me come, Caine."

I pat his hard stomach. "Isn't that the goal?"

Jon laughs like a child. "Not yet." He rolls us both over so that he is straddling me again. "Can I sit on your dick?"

I assume he can't see my shock in this darkness. I reach into the nightstand and fumble for condoms and a bottle of lube without a word. I pull a condom over my cock and lube it up, certain I am getting more lube on the sheets than my cock. I grab his cock like a handle and pull him forward. I feel him reaching behind as he maneuvers against me until we are finally lined up.

My eyes have adjusted to the dark enough to see Jon staring down at me. I'm tempted to push my way in, but force myself to allow him to take his time. He exhales with a slight whistle as he slowly pushes down on me. My hands are on his chest, feeling his muscles tense as he slides down my shaft. His ass is a furnace.

"Fuck," He gasps.

"It hurts a little at first."

"A little? Jesus, dude. It feels like you're tearing me in half."

I massage his chest, wishing I could see his face better. "Want to stop?"

"Nope," he says without hesitation. His hands move to my

5

chest. "Just give me a minute."

"You can sit on my dick like this all month if you want."

That makes him laugh. "Should we wake Glenn?"

"Your call, buddy. He would love this."

He shifts his weight, pressing on my chest. "This is my first time with a dude. Two of you may be overwhelming."

I nod. "Like I said; totally your call."

He hovers there for a minute, teasing me until I can no longer resist. I grab his small waist and begin pushing.

"Fuck," he cries out. "I can't do it. I can't do it."

I freeze in place and wait, but Jon doesn't pull away from me. I push a little, slowly, allowing Jon every opportunity to stop me. He pats my chest without a word in what I assume is a sign to continue. He exhales as I push a little more. I continue pushing until he trembles, then slowly thrust my hips. He grips my chest and moans, yet doesn't pull away or try to stop me. I pump harder as he begins to relax, loving the little yelps he makes each time I go deep.

I wish Glenn would wake up and join us.

Jon's lips brush up against mine. I ask if he is okay and see him nod. I wrap my hand around his neck and push him to the side, rolling with him until he is on his back and pinned under me. Still inside him, I push his knees to his chest and begin slamming his ass just like Glenn likes me to fuck him. He makes this wonderful sound with each thrust, a combination of a yelp and a gasp. He tries reaching under his leg to jack off, but I push his hand away and continue pumping. His breaths become shallow gasps.

The hallway nightlight is finally enough for me to see his sharp blue eyes boring into mine. He grasps both my biceps as though clinging for life. He nods, quickly, and begins moaning. "Oh, fuuuuuck" he grunts as he shoots a massive load without even touching his dick, a load so heavy I can hear it splashing all over his chest. A second shot of cum goes over his head to thump against the headboard and the third dumps across his neck and pools onto the sheets. His look of horrified wonder brings me over the edge. I pull out of his tight ass with a pop, rip the condom off, and shoot my load all over his wet belly with a spastic grunt. Spent, I collapse on him without care of the mess we are making as we pant in silence.

"Fuck," he finally groans.

"Damned right," I laugh as I roll off from him. I use the crumbled-up sheet to wipe cum and sweat from his chest. We lay like this for a few minutes and I watch the shadow of his smooth chest rise and fall as he sinks into sleep. I swear he's smiling.

The sounds of Jon's soft breathing and Glenn's distant snoring envelope me as I begin drifting off to sleep. I guess Glenn was right about Jon. Good for him, and good for me. Maybe the three of us can have more fun like this in the morning.

Reflecting back on that moment, I was filled with enthusiasm about what the future held for Glenn, Jon, and me. I don't think I've ever made such a poor assessment of a situation before.

That was the last night I slept in our apartment.

CHAPTER TWO

I still ache from yesterday's eleven-hour drive from Albuquerque. I spent last night in a cheap little motel in Indio and am excited to check into the guest house I booked online for my thirteen-week stay here in Palm Springs. I turn over and reach for Glenn out of habit, but I haven't seen him in thirty-four days.

I thought Glenn wanted to actually kill me after he woke to find Jon in our bed. I've known Glenn since our days in varsity wrestling at Rio Rancho High and while he's always been a little high-strung, I've never seen him so mad. He lost his shit, but I still don't understand why. Jon grabbed his clothes and scrambled out of our apartment without a sound as Glenn began throwing furniture and knocking over our book shelves. He was screaming about how I should be ashamed for cheating on him in our own bed. I tried reasoning with Glenn, reminding him he created the situation and that we were all drunk, but anything I said further enraged him. His face was red with anger and he looked like a child: I couldn't help but laugh at his ridiculous behavior. That's when he did something I never expected: he punched me in the face, grazing my left cheek without really connecting. I've never hit anyone before and considered hitting him back, but in a split second I reasoned Glenn is a well-trained cop who could have done serious damage had he really wanted to. Glenn was my first boyfriend and, until that night, the only man I had ever been with. I'm not sure if I actually loved him, but I certainly cared for him and loved our time together. The man who stood in front of me that night was a complete stranger and I knew in that moment I wanted nothing more from him. I remember stuffing clothes and essentials in a few grocery bags and stepping out of our apartment without a word.

That was five weeks ago. I haven't seen Glenn, nor Jon for that matter, since that day.

I knew I had to leave New Mexico after two nights at my parents' home under the disapproving glare of my father. I came out to my parents right after high school and while my mother seemed fine with the information in her passive way, my father took it as a personal attack against his masculinity to have a queer son. Eight years have passed and my father still refuses to disguise his shame in my "life choices and priorities". I've learned over the years to pretend not to care what he thinks of me. I'm still learning, I guess.

I've been a critical care nurse at a small hospital in Albuquerque for the past four years and took a chance by applying for several travel nursing positions. A recruiter in Phoenix found an ICU position in Palm Springs. After several weeks of credentialing, background checks, drug screens and telephone interviews, I was able to make my escape plan. I'm still not sure what I've gotten myself into, but my salary during this thirteen-week contract is more than double what I made in Albuquerque. The recruiter took care of extending my nursing license to California and helped me find a place to stay.

Note to self: I need to send my recruiter, Desmond, some sort of thank you gift.

The motel bed creaks as I stretch my arms over my head with a yawn. I'm horny and I stink. Indio is part of the Coachella valley which includes Palm Springs, Rancho Mirage, Palm Desert and some other cities I've never heard of. It is roughly ninety minutes inland from Los Angeles and, apparently, ripe with gay sex. While I suspect the best way to put Glenn and his bullshit behind me would be to hook up with someone else, I don't have the psychological energy this morning. Five weeks have passed and it still feels weird to even consider having sex without Glenn.

I pull my dick out of my underwear and begin a long session of boy-stuff. I don't know if it's the smell of the cheap hotel or the fact I finally have privacy, but I've been horned like a bull since I got here last night. I'm jacking off to the image of Jon at that moment right before he came, remembering the amazing sounds he made each time I pushed deep inside him. My eyes roll back as I imagine him roped spread-eagle on the bed, face down and ass up, helpless. I've never tried any form of bondage, but roping a man down is always my go-to image while masturbating. I can almost smell the sharp saltiness of Jon and our loads comingled on his sweaty chest. I imagine what it would have been like if Glenn had found us in bed and joined us rather than freaking out, of how hot it would have been to fuck Jon together. The image of Glenn fucking Jon pushes an orgasm so violent my ass aches afterwards.

I wipe globs of sticky cum from my stomach with the hand towel I used for the same purpose twice last night. I can't say for sure that I miss Glenn, but I miss us having sex every morning.

I have no idea if I will ever see him again.

I don't know if that matters.

I'm twenty-six years old and here in the California desert for the next thirteen weeks. I can't think of any reason to dwell on the past at this point. I will worry about the next step when I need to.

I'm ready for the next adventure.

It's 92 degrees in mid-April as I pull up to what will be my home for the next three months. Similar to Albuquerque, most of the homes here have stonework and desert landscaping rather than lawns. This house is one of dozens or so tract homes on a wide, curved street. I spoke to my new landlords on the phone and even face-timed with them several times during the past few weeks. They seem very cool. Mitch is a Realtor and Stephani is a corporate event planner. They said they often travel and offered me a great rate on their detached guest room/pool house provided I watch their dogs when they are out of town.

A petite, middle-aged woman whom I assume is Stephani

steps out from the house. She's wearing white pants, a dark blue blouse, and sunglasses far too large for her face. Her dark hair is pulled back in a braid and she is all smile.

"You must be Caine," she shouts as she works her way down the long walkway. "You made it."

"You're stuck with me now," I regret saying as soon as it came out of my mouth. I step forward and shake her hand.

"We were worried, being Friday the 13th and all." Her tone tells me she is kidding. She's much shorter than I had imagined but, then, I question why I imagined her any particular height. I'm six foot even so she must be 5'1" at best. I open the hatch of my Countryman and retrieve my suitcase and gym bag. Stephani glances at my empty trunk and my back seat. "This is all you brought?"

I nod. "I wasn't sure what I needed aside from my scrubs and gym clothes."

She nods quickly. "Sure, sure. The guest house is completely furnished and we can help you shop for whatever you need. Let me show you your place."

I follow her into their large living room which looks out to their pool and am immediately attacked by three cheerful little dogs. I set down my suitcase to greet them. "They're shy, I see."

"I know. They make terrible guard-dogs but they are so damned sweet."

"Miniature greyhounds?"

"Italian Greyhounds. The tan one is Vinnie; he's the crazy one. The grey one is Bruno, and the brown one is Rocco. Boys! Go outside!" She opens the sliding glass door and they look at her sideways like she's crazy. Stephani shakes her head and leads me outside, remarking on basic landmarks such as the barbeque and firepit as we pass around the pool and enter the guest house.

There's nothing fancy about this small guest house, but I love it as soon as I step through the French doors. The main room consisting of a small kitchen, dining area and living room is painted pale grey with bright white crown molding and rust-colored curtains opening to large windows facing their private back yard. There is a bedroom and bathroom in another room which is similarly appointed but much darker.

Stephani points out everything she thinks I need to know before stepping outside. "You must be exhausted after your long drive so I'll let you rest."

I don't know why I don't tell her I arrived in the area last night and am well-rested.

She glances at my small suitcase. "Unpacking won't take you five minutes so feel free to nap, use the pool or explore the city. I have some work to complete and Mitch should be home around five. We'd love you to join us for cocktails before we head out to that dreadful party in Upland I told you about."

I thank her and unpack. She was right about it only taking five minutes, so I change into my only bathing suit, grab one of the pool towels from the bathroom, and take her up on her offer to swim. The pool is warmer than I'd imagined but feels great in this baking sun. I swim a few laps, then lift myself out of the pool and arrange the towel on one of several lounges encircling the pool. The sun feels amazing and my skin dries in minutes. There's a soft breeze and I'm about to fall asleep when Stephani steps back into the yard.

"I don't mean to mother you, though I'm old enough to be your mother, but—oh, someone works out."

I sit up and smile.

"I really think you should use sunscreen." She displays a plastic basket filled with a dozen different options. "Your skin tone is so light; are you Scandinavian?"

"Italian/Norwegian, so I can tan. It just takes a while."

"Ha, I was half right. Here," she displays a tube of lotion, "I recommend spf 75 the first few weeks." She begins applying lotion to my arms and shoulders in a completely non-sexual way. "Here," she hands me the lotion, "turn around and put some on your legs while I do your back. Don't forget your feet."

"Thank you." She begins massaging lotion into my back, which feels amazing. I should be humiliated, but she is being very sweet and I can't recall the last time my mother touched me like this.

She pats my back, clearly finished. "Don't worry; sweetheart: you'll darken up in a few weeks just like the rest of us." She walks back into the main house, leaving me to soak in the warmth. My smooth chest shines with lotion and I rub my hands over my flexed abs until I start getting horny and have to stop touching myself.

I look at my cellphone: No messages. It's not like I want to talk to Glenn, but it feels so weird he isn't reaching out. I expected something by now, even if just to tell me he hates me. I set a timer for thirty minutes before rolling over on my stomach to allow my back equal time. After that, I take a shower. Changing into cargo shorts and a tank top, and read an eBook on my phone in the shade created by the covered porch which runs the length of the guest house.

I look up from my reading a few hours later as Mitch steps into the back yard. I think I gasp and feel the fool as I stand up to great him. I've seen his face plenty of times but never realized he is such a fucking stud. He's probably 5'11 with a worked-out body, wavy brown hair, dark brown eyes and perfect teeth. He's wearing nothing but pale blue speedos and has one of those bulges that, well, why would he wear anything but speedos with that going on. I do my best to look at his eyes but am pretty sure I am staring at his furry chest.

Who wouldn't buy a house from this guy?

He takes my offered hand with a firm grip and introduces himself. "Join us for happy hour?" His voice is deep yet soft, with a little bit of an accent I can't place and hadn't notice over the phone.

I want to tell him I'd join him for anything. Instead, I nod like a dork and pretend not to glance at his speedos.

"Great, let me just cool off right quick." Mitch turns and dives into the pool, moving effortless through the water. I pretend I'm not watching him.

I'm so glad I'm wearing sunglasses.

Stephani joins us with a tray of drinks and some fruit. "I

poured Campari and soda without even asking what you like to drink. I can make you something else if you prefer."

I have no idea what Campari is but it looks fun so I take the offered glass with a smile. I can feel the change in gravity as Mitch rises out of the pool and stands, dripping, behind me. I can't bring myself to face him. His arm reaches around me to take the glass Stephani hands him and they both clink their glasses against mine. "Happy Friday the 13th," she sings.

"Here's to new friendships," Mitch adds from behind.

I mumble something and sip my drink, which tastes like cough medicine and club soda. It has an interesting after-taste and is surprisingly refreshing. I don't hate it.

Mitch grabs my right bicep and I almost blow my load. "Your arms are huge. Do you have a local gym membership yet?"

"I don't, and thanks."

"I can hook you up at World Gym if you like."

I take another sip and remove my glasses before turning to face him. "That would be great."

I don't know why I get so nervous around older men, whether they be my dad, a doctor, or a random salesman. Interacting with them makes me feel like a little boy. We chat through two more rounds of drinks (they are calling a car service tonight) and I learn how they met and a bunch of blah blah blah I can't pay attention to. Mitch looks intoxicating so I do my best to focus on Stephani. It's not working. Mitch is generating an electric current I can't escape and I fear my attraction is obvious. I have to pull my shit together.

At least I have good jack-off material to keep me busy for the next three months.

CHAPTER THREE

I completed my week of orientation at the hospital and have the weekend off. Stephani and Mitch invited me to an all-day hike tomorrow but I told them I made plans with one of the nurses I'd met. That was a lie, but I can't be around a sweaty Mitch for a full day without going crazy.

That being said, I feel it's finally time for a little post-Glenn action. I need something to make me stop thinking about him, and I doubt my straight landlord is going to help me out. It's nine on a Friday night and I'm guessing anyone who wants to be somewhere is already there, but who knows? It's hard to wrap my mind around the fact I've only had sex with Glenn, Jon, and that girl from High School. I log onto a gay hook-up site with that profile I made last week and begin the search for someone to be my number four.

My profile isn't over-the-top: twenty-six, six foot, one-hundred-eighty pounds, brown hair and eyes. My stats are listed as forty-eight chest, thirty-four waist, Italian/Norwegian, eight inches, cut. My primary photo is a little dorky and I'm wearing a Lobos hat, but I also posted the photo Stephani took of me sleeping by the pool all oiled up and looking more muscular than I am. She told me I should send the photo to my mom and show her how relaxed I am. Sorry, mom, but I have other plans for this photo.

I respond politely to several guys before coming across Juan Miguel's profile. I've seen the Cuban adult film star in dozens of porn scenes and think he lives in Florida. He's either visiting Palm Springs or, more likely, this is some asshole using his photo. I send him a simple message: *how's it going tonight, handsome?*

I'm good, he replies rather quickly. *Bored and a little horny.*

That gets a rise from my eyebrows as well as my dick. *Same here.*

You a top? he responds. *I'd love you to fuck me tonight.*

That surprises me on several levels: one; Juan Miquel is always a big rough top in his movies. Two; he is stunningly beautiful and I'm not sure what he expects from me. I'm leaning more and more into doubting this is really him.

Total top here, I type back.

We message back and forth a few times until I stop caring who this guy really is: he seems fun and chill and I just want to meet someone who may help me get over the whole Glenn situation. Before I know how it happens, I have his address. *What's your name?* I ask. I'm not sure why and I fear it may offend him, but I am embarrassed to admit I recognize his photos. Recognize, hell: I've shot loads to his scenes hundreds of times to the point Glenn used to call Juan Miguel my other boyfriend.

He says his name is Rik and gives me the code to access the back gate to a house not far from here. He says we can have some fun in the pool house. Pool houses are apparently the thing here in the desert. *I can be there in forty-five minutes.*

I take a quick shower, put on clean underwear, gym shorts and a t-shirt, and make it to the backyard of what looks like a billionaire's compound right on time. I type in the gate code and walk through the back yard to the well-lite pool house as instructed. The main house looks like a marble hotel and seems acres across the yard. I knock on the pool house door.

Juan Miguel opens the door wearing sweats and an old wife beater which shows off his tight body. I know at once it is actually him and am surprised by his height, or lack thereof: he has to be five-seven at best. I'm also surprised he looks much better than he does in his movies; and even more muscular. His famous wavy brown hair is cropped short and his gray eyes look tired. If I didn't know better, I would guess he is shy or nervous. He beckons me in and starts making polite small talk.

This pool house is very different from the one I'm staying in: the vaulted ceiling must be twenty feet high and the floors and walls are white marble. There's a huge four-poster bed in the middle of the long rectangular room with a kitchen on one side and a living room on the other. The room is relatively dark aside from a light over the bed. It looks like a stage.

I know I'm out of my league here so I decide to gamble. I grab the front of his neck while he is still chatting about something and pull him toward me, kissing him before he can stop me. I think I catch him off guard because he gasps but doesn't pull away. I kiss him harder and begin rubbing his muscular shoulders. He's tense at first, then sighs and seems to relax.

I figure I better move fast before he changes his mind and asks me to leave, so I reach down and grab the back of his thighs and pick him up like a child to carry him to the bed. His eyes—damn, those eyes—and the way he grips my arms tell me this is exactly what he wants. I drop him on the bed and pull his sweats off to find he's wearing a ragged red jockstrap. He rolls over on his stomach to show off his ass; smooth and tight with no tan line.

I can't believe I am in a bed with Juan Miquel. I slowly climb onto the bed and lean forward toward his beautiful ass as though being drawn to it. I lick it, lightly, causing him to arch his back. My little bites make him moan. I grab his hips and pull him to the end of the bed, burying my face in his ass.

"Aye, Papi. Yes" he whispers in his beautiful Cuban accent as he spreads his legs into near splits. He acts as though no one has ever worshiped him like this before, which is very unlikely.

I've spent hundreds of nights jacking off while imagining this very scene, so I make it last. I eat his sweet ass, lapping at his hole and chewing on his taint until my jaw is sore and he is writhing like a cat. I work his ass until he's making a deep moaning sound which drives me mad.

I simply can't wait any longer.

I yank my shorts and underwear down to my ankles in one hard pull and climb on top of him. Wrapping my hands around the back of his neck, I force his head into the mattress with my weight. "I'm sorry," I say in true sincerity, "but I have to fuck you." I spit on his ass and grind my cock between his vice-like cheeks.

He moans and assumes a push-up stance, grinding his ass against my cock. I reach behind his right thigh and push his knee up towards his chest, spread his cheeks apart, and spit on his ass again. His entire body goes limp as soon as the head of my cock connects with his hole.

I take this as a sign of consent and surrender. There are condoms in my shorts but I can't force myself away from this connection. I continue pressing against his hole as a warning, giving him the opportunity to stop me. I'm highly aware I should ask permission before entering him raw, but Juan Miguel is mine in this instant and I have to be inside him. I push in, slow but unrelenting. His hole is fevered and tight. His moans seem real and I worry he may need more than spit as lube because I don't want to do anything to ruin this moment. I move slowly for a few minutes, indulging in his tight grip on my pulsing cock. Time moves slow as he begins to relax his grip. I push deeper inside, gasping at the sensation. His hole squeezes my cock with each beat of his heart, working my cock until I am moaning without restraint. I wrap my arms under and around him, inhaling his scent as I hold him prisoner in this position as long as I can bear.

"All good," I whisper in the ear I am chewing.

"This is perfect." His accent has faded away, something I place in my "interesting but address later" file. "I am yours."

I slowly pull my cock out before shoving it back in.

"Easy with me, boy."

I pull completely out again before ramming my cock back into place.

He punches the bed and growls something in Spanish.

He's pretty built for such a small guy, so I'm confident he can pull away from me if he wants. I take the fact he hasn't punched me as a green light. I pull out and slam into him, again and again, each time causing his moan to become more of a groan. His voice gets deeper and deeper with each movement until I am reeling and feel stoned.

All pretenses vanish and I can't bother faking concern for his pleasure. I pull away long enough to rip his wife-beater to shreds, revealing the infamous tattoos all over his back. I lap at the hard line between his back muscles like a dog as my cock locks in on its target. Squeezing his head between my hands, I begin pounding his ass as hard as I can. He shouts out each time I go deep, his hands clutching mine in an ecstatic frenzy. I put my weight into it and fuck him hard and long until I am panting. Sweat pours off my body as I jackhammer his ass. It becomes animal in this moment and he is nothing more than a hole for me to use. His words are wild and indecipherable, the language of fuck.

I continue slamming his ass until there is absolutely no possibility of stopping myself from unloading. My first shot drives deep and I fear I may pass out as I continue pumping my load. "Fuck. Fuck," I keep growling, unable to stop as I ride out my convulsive orgasm. "Fuuuuuuuuuuuck!"

The world stops and my body hums with energy. The salty smell of sex fills my lungs. My heartbeat fills my ears. We are connected at this moment by more than just my cock.

Time begins again. I am panting in his ear and showering him with sweat.

He wiggles his ass from side to side, generating undulating waves of euphoria. After what seems like hours, he slides out from under me and smiles, showing off bright white teeth. He wipes sweat from my face. "Are you able to do that again?"

"Sure," I pant, completely wrecked. "Just give me a few weeks to recharge."

"Good," someone says from behind us.

The voice is like a shot of a gun and I leap to my feet to find a dark-haired man sitting in a chair at the end of the room. Had he been there the whole time?

"What?" I say, covering my dick with my hands.

"I said good," the man says. "He deserves more of that."

"Who the hell is he?" I ask Juan Miguel, or Rik, or whatever his name is.

"My husband."

"Oh shit," I back away from the bed. "I'm sorry."

"Don't be," the stranger says with a smile. "You were wonderful."

"Oh," is all I manage. This is so fucking weird. I don't know what to do or say. I just want to bolt.

Rik gets up from the bed and goes around a corner to what I assume is a bathroom.

"Don't tell me you regret it," the man says from the shadows.

"Embarrassed."

"Honey, what do you have to be embarrassed about? Look at you: you're absolutely beautiful."

"I'm sorry, I'm at such a loss here."

"I'm Liam, Rik's husband, partner and Sir."

"Uh …, hi. I'm Caine."

"You're Caine and Abel, very able."

I glance around, wondering where my shorts are. "Should I leave?"

Rik returns and brushes his fingers across my bare ass as he walks past me. He's wearing the jock strap again. "Liam, you are making him uncomfortable. Be nice." He turns to face me. "Don't let him fool you, sexy boy. My husband is one of the nicest men you will ever meet."

Liam stands and steps into the light. He looks to be mid-forties with short brown hair, dark eyes, and a well-kept beard. He's wearing a black polo shirt tucked into jeans, a thick black belt with an ornate buckle, and black boots. He's a little shorter than me and somewhat pudgy, but he has a nice chest and wide shoulders which balances it out. "Can we offer you a drink?"

I need ten but refrain from sharing that detail. I nod.

"I'm getting high on the testosterone coursing through here," Liam say as he steps closer. His eyes are actually a dark shade of green and there is a soft kindness in his smile. "Let's go to the main house."

"Will the owners mind?

"Honey, where did you come from?"

"Albuquerque," I mumble stupidly.

Liam wraps an arm around Rik and beckons me to follow

them. "We don't mind at all."

CHAPTER FOUR

I pull on my shorts, leaving my underwear and shirt on the marbled floor, and follow Liam and Rik through the extensive backyard past a lake of a pool towards the main house. I'm ready for Leonardo DiCaprio to step out and greet us like a scene from "The Great Gatsby". They lead me to a covered patio which looks like a nightclub and encourage me to sit in one of the twenty barstools surrounding the sunken bar. Rik sits next to me as Liam circles around the bar to face us.

"What's your poison?"

"Uh," I hate how often I stammer when nervous. "What do you have?"

"Everything."

I pause, which makes Rik laugh. He rubs my arm. "Don't be shy, Daddy. What do you like to drink?"

"Daddy?"

"Yes, yes; you're younger than I am. You are Daddy as long as I can still feel you inside of me, yes?"

The image makes my cock twitch. "Fair enough." I turn back to Liam. "May I have a gin and tonic."

"Making it easy on me. And here I worried you were one of those complicated men."

I glance around the surrounding luxury. "Sorry, I'm not very fancy."

Liam stares at me for a moment and smiles. "That's perfect."

"Where did you grow up?" Rik asks without a hint of his Cuban accent.

"I was born in Rio Rancho, a little north of Albuquerque, but I've been living in Albuquerque for the past few years." I explain the situation with my place at Mitch and Stephani's.

Liam hands me the drink and then pours himself a glass of white wine. He hands Rik a bottle of water. "Are you in the adult film industry?"

"No," I laugh. "God no." I look at Rik, "No offense."

Rik laughs.

"Why?"

"You're built like a porn star."

"He fucks like a porn star," Rik adds, rubbing his ass.

"That's funny, as you're only the fourth person I've had sex with?"

"This week?"

"Ever."

Liam pretends to choke on his wine. "You almost made me spill my drink.

I apologize, causing both to laugh. Liam watches me as I explain my history with Glenn, that night with Jon, and my decision to leave Albuquerque for a new start.

"The reason I asked if you were in porn," Liam says out of nowhere, "is because you walk around like a timid little boy yet fuck with such confidence."

"Porn stars are timid?"

Liam nods. "Many are, yes. They hide it behind their sexuality." Liam stares at me again. "You're a little boy in a man's body. You haven't figured out who you are."

I take a sip. "I suppose not. But I'm twenty-six. I'm not a boy."

Rik rubs my cock through my shorts "And he's not little."

"First," Liam says, holding up his hand. "I meant no disrespect. Second, age has nothing to do with being a boy. We've met boys in their fifties and men in their twenties."

I take another sip, feeling naked in Liam's gaze. "I should have used a condom."

"Yes. Rik is HIV negative and on PreP."

I'm surprised when neither of them asks my HIV status. "I tested negative last month. I'm not taking PreP."

"Maybe you should."

PreP is an acronym for the HIV pre-exposure prophylaxis medication which decreases the chance of infection. It's not a medication they teach in nursing school, but I assume most gay men are familiar with it.

"Especially," Liam continues, "if you are going to make a habit of barebacking strangers."

"Oh my god."

Liam seems to enjoy my discomfort. "I'm teasing. You have questions."

Interesting that he says that as a statement rather than a question. My father taught me never to disrespect someone by asking what they do for work or how they make their money—then again, he also taught me to hate myself for being gay. I skip the obvious questions and turn to Rik. "Your accent?"

"I give people what I think they want. Juan Miguel has an accent, but my family moved to Miami from Cuba when I was five. I grew up in the United States and no longer have such an accent in my real life."

"Real life? Juan Miguel is your fake life?"

"Absolutely. I have a degree in interior design and haven't done porn in ten years, but most people only choose to see their fantasy of me. It's silly, when you think about it. If I worked as a waiter ten years ago, would people ask if I still wait tables on the side?"

I nod, turning to Liam. "What did you mean when you said you are Rik's husband, partner and Sir?"

Liam is leaning on the bar's marble countertop but stands straight, eyebrows raised. "Now that's a fun question. We are legally married, so he is my husband. We are equals in business, so he is my partner. Rik is also, unlike his film persona, a submissive bondage masochist. Therefore, I am also his Sir."

My dick twitches at the mention of bondage. "So, he's like …, your slave?"

Both laugh at my apparent misstep. "Not a slave, no. We have a slave under contract which makes us both his Master, but that's another story."

"I'm confused."

Rik hops off a barstool and pats my leg. "I'll be right back."

Liam studies me. "Fetish life is confusing to most people, especially as it's portrayed so horribly wrong in movies—"

"Fifty shades of blah," Rik yells out from across the yard.

"Exactly. I am a true BDSM Master, something I was taught when I was no older than you."

"BDSM," I repeat.

"An abbreviated acronym for B/D, which is bondage and discipline; D/S, which is dominance and submission; and S/M, which is sadism and masochism. However, the term BDSM has grown over the years to apply to a number of erotic acts and roles."

I nod. "I've used the term before in reference to bondage, but never knew what the acronym actually stood for. Bondage has always turned me on."

Liam leans forward. "Elaborate."

I shrug, a bad habit I catch myself doing far too often. "You know, the typical stuff. A sexy man with his hands roped behind his back. Someone being overpowered. Someone helpless."

"And which role do you prefer in these scenarios?"

I sip my drink. It tastes great, but I'm milking it because I have to drive home. "Do you mean, like, do I want to be roped down or do I want to be the one roping someone down."

"Yes."

"I don't think I'd like being bound."

"You want to be in control."

I nod.

"You fantasize about taking control of powerful men because you feel out of control in your real life."

"Uh, I don't know about that.

Liam nods. "Yes. You do."

I finish my drink and cover it with my hand when Liam asks if I'd like another. "Do you have a specialty, fetish-wise?"

"My specialty," Liam winks at Rik as he rejoins us, "if I had to choose one aspect, is sadism. Administering pain to others, both physically as well as psychologically, turns me on."

"Wow."

"Let me put it another way: I am drawn to those who become aroused by pain and humiliation. It has to be consensual. I wouldn't get off on bringing you down to our dungeon and beating you with a paddle unless that turned you on. I mean, I probably would enjoy it, but it's not something I am interested in. Rather, I want someone who begs me to spank them, who begs me to humiliate them: someone who truly derives pleasure from pain. Does that make sense?"

I nod, allowing him to watch me.

"I'm not what you expected of a bondage master."

It's as though he can read my mind. "No."

"What did you expect" Bigger, older?"

"You're just so …, nice. Normal."

Liam nods. "Most people you meet who claim to be dominants or masters are driven by ego: they want to demonstrate power over another to compensate for their powerlessness in life. A true master is never selfish, never expects an imbalanced power exchange. Take Rik here."

"Yes, please. Take me."

"Stop," Liam scolds without intent. "Rik is a true submissive."

I assess the beautiful porn star standing next to me. "You were always such a brute in your movies."

"Again, that wasn't me, really. Contrary to what most people believe, we really are acting during those scenes."

I nod, taking it all in.

"Being submissive doesn't mean he is weak or powerless," Liam continues. "Rather, it means he is drawn to submitting to my will for our mutual satisfaction. Even our slave holds power in the exchange, though that gets more complicated than simple dominance and submission."

"It sounds very complicated."

"Ecstasy dwells in the complication of life." Liam says as though it explains everything.

"You said you have a dungeon?"

Liam laughs. "Want to see it?"

I hesitate.

"Caine, my fine young man: you are perfectly safe here…, unless Rik decides to cook for us"

"Hush, you." Rik says with a smile

"Do you trust me?"

I have no reason for it, but I absolutely do. I nod and follow them into the main house. We pass through a large room with a pool table and a wall-sized television I would love to hook my Xbox to. Shit, I suppose that's Glenn's Xbox now. Oh well.

Liam and Rik lead me down rather tight spiral stairs to a plain white door. Liam looks at me and smirks. "Disappointed?"

I shrug. "I don't know what I expected, a door like a bank vault or something?"

"That's not a bad idea, but no. This was originally a wine cellar." Liam removes keys from his jeans and unlocks the door.

"Wait, it locks from the outside."

Rik pokes my belly with his index finger. My dick thrums with life every time he touches me. "Can't have our slaves running free now, can we?"

"What if we get locked in?"

Liam shakes the keys at me. "The door unlocks from both sides, and you're big enough to bust it down if needed."

I step into a large square room smelling of leather and candle wax. The floor is soft rubber tiles like you'd find in a gym and the walls and ceiling are painted a flat dark grey. In the dead center of the room is a huge steel-framed canopy bondage bed. There's a large red-leather X-shaped device attached to the foot of the bed extending from the floor to the top of the canopy, something I recognize from movies as a device to strap people to in various positions. I can't help running my fingers across it as I walk by.

The walls to the left and right of the door are lined with hooks and shelves from which hundreds of items such as whips, paddles and other sex toys—for lack of a better term—are displayed. The back wall is a jail cell approximately 6 feet deep which runs the width of the room, containing metal bunk beds and a stainless-steel toilet.

"Does the toilet function?"

"Need to piss?

I laugh, trying to not sound nervous. "Naw, just curious."

"It does, yes." Liam steps behind me as I attempt to identify various paraphernalia encompassing the room. "What catches your attention?

"All of it. It's overwhelming, almost."

Liam chuckles. "Which item draws your attention the most?"

I can't help notice a huge black dildo in the shape of a human arm topped by an exaggeratedly large fist, but I play it safe and point at a leather paddle.

"I win!" Rik says. He steps up to the leather X, spreads his legs and grabs metal rings on the top portions I hadn't noticed before. He shakes his sexy little ass back and forth.

Liam hands me the paddle. It's heavier than I imagined, maybe metal wrapped in black leather, and is probably eighteen inches long and six wide. I sniff it, which makes one of Liam's eyebrows bounce. "Really?"

I shrug and feel myself blush. "The smell of leather has always turned me on."

Liam rests a hand on my arm and looks deep into me. "Never be ashamed of your passion.

I nod, numb.

Liam points to Rik's playful ass. "Try it out."

"Spank him?"

"Whatever you want. Isn't that right, Rik?"

"Hurt me, Papito." Juan Miguel and his accent have returned. "Punish me. I've been baaaad."

"Normally," Liam says as I approach Rik. "I would recommend restraining the person before a session. Rik, however, is a professional and won't move unless instructed."

I bounce the paddle in my right hand and swing it around a few times like you would a tennis racket, then swat him once across his right cheek. I kind of miss the mark and hit his hip.

"Aye!" Rik yelps.

"So much for being timid," Liam says with a big laugh.

"I'm sorry, did I—"

"Never apologize. Rik loves it, and I told you you're safe here. Try again."

I swat him again, aiming better and with much less force. Still, Rik's flesh jumps with the impact and a yelp escapes his lips. This paddle is wicked. I swat him again in the same place, leaving a rectangular red mark across his flawless skin. Three more swats, each consecutively harder, leaving Rik panting. Three more times, then five—I like odd numbers—and sweat breaks out across his tatted back. I look to Liam for indication I should back off, but he nods encouragement. Five more times, then five in the opposite direction across his left cheek. I trace the welt forming on his ass with my index finger, making Rik hop up and down. "Does that hurt or feel good?"

"Yes."

I drop to my knees and set the paddle beside me. I lick the reddening welt across his ass, which pulsates and is much warmer than his unmarked skin. I'm fascinated; lost for words. I rub his ass and work my hands up his back until I am standing behind him. I stand there a few minutes, pressing against him. I would fuck him again if I had the energy. Instead, I step away and give him a final slap with my hand.

"You're a fun one," Rik turns around, rubbing his ass. "Ooh, I'm not sitting for a while."

"I'm—" I stop myself from apologizing. "This is surreal."

"Caine, you are welcome to stay and play with Rik all you like, but I need to be up early tomorrow." Liam glances at his watch. "Well, today."

So tempting. What if I never get another opportunity to do this? But, no. "Thank you so much, but I should head back."

Rik pulls a wipe from a purple container similar to the chlorhexidine wipes we use in hospitals and cleans the paddle before returning it to its hook. Liam leads us back upstairs.

Reaching into a cabinet at the top of the stairs, he hands me a small box. "A gift."

I take it, embarrassed. "Thank you. What is it?"

"Leather-scented candle. Burn it the next time you masturbate."

I open the box to find a small candle jar. I pop off the lid and give it a sniff. It smells just like the paddle. "Amazing."

"A friend of ours owns a company here in town that makes them. We'll introduce you someday."

I give them both a big hug, then feel stupid for not having fought the impulse.

"Such a sweet boy," Liam says as I pull away from him.

"He's not so sweet with a paddle."

I start to walk out the back patio when Liam grabs my arm. "Caine, you can use the front door."

"Oh, right. But my shorts are still in the pool house."

Rik points to a Trader Joe's paper bag. "I grabbed your stuff while Liam was making you a drink. I'm keeping your underwear, though."

"Uh, oh. Okay."

Rik pushes between us, rubbing against me, and kisses my neck. "Call it a souvenir."

I can't help but wonder how many men have left their underwear in this mansion as they lead me through the dining room to a large entrance hall with a black massive staircase. I hug them both again at the door.

"What an amazing night."

"Consider it your introduction to fetish, your first lesson."

"My first? There will be others?"

Liam pulls me down by the back of my neck and gives me a sweet kiss. It's the kind of kiss a friend would give you, but it still makes my cock groan. "Absolutely."

CHAPTER FIVE

Three weeks have passed since that night with Liam and Rik. Since then, they have taken me to dinner at several of their favorite places: all nicer than any restaurant I have been yet casual enough so that we could wear shorts and t-shirts. I'm learning Palm Springs can be summed up as "casual elegance" with a disturbingly large presence of homeless people. I've noticed the town attracts tourists from all over the world as well as huge crowds of young gay people from Los Angeles and San Diego each weekend. The resident gays, however, tend to be older and suspiciously wealthy. They are also much more muscular than the guys in Albuquerque.

Work has been difficult and there is a particular doctor at this hospital who seems to hate me for whatever reason, but the money is great. I keep telling myself I can do anything for this kind of money when it is only three shifts a week. I spend my days off working out at Mitch's gym and catching up on recreational reading: I'm currently on book three of a large series from my favorite science fiction writer. I have today off and am pretending to read this book in my hand. In reality, I am watching Mitch's chest rise and fall as he sleeps on a lounge by the pool. His speedo is red today.

My phone vibrates. It is a text from Liam. *Are you working today?*

Nope. I have today and tomorrow off.

Are you jacking off to you landlord again?

I swear he's psychic. I take a quick photo of Mitch, crop it, and send it to Liam.

Christ on a stick.

I told you. I can't stop staring at him. It's so embarrassing.

A man as beautiful as that should be stared at. Also, I told you not to feel shame for your passion. It seems we need to liberate you from your shame.

I'm uncertain what he means, but I respond with a smiley emote.

The time has come for lesson number two, Liam texts.

Does it involve sitting on Mitch's face?

Calm down, tiger. Report to the Caliente Tropics hotel room 208 at exactly 8:05 tonight. The door will be unlocked. Knock twice, wait 30 seconds, and then let yourself in and lock the door behind you. There will be two envelopes on the bed marked number one and number two. Read number one immediately and save number two for right before you are ready to leave. The room and everything in it are yours for two hours. Call me when you're done.

The message was obviously a copy and paste as he couldn't possibly have typed that quickly, and I can't help ponder how many people Liam has sent this message to in the past. *Hey, what if I was working tomorrow?*

Then you would be tired tomorrow.

My dick bounces in nervous excitement and I have a dozen questions I want to ask, but I respond with a simple *Yes, Sir.*

I stare at my phone for several minutes before realizing the conversation is complete. It's six-thirty on a hot Thursday evening and I stink of pool water and sweat. I look up the hotel and see it is a ten-minute drive, giving me more than enough time for a shower.

I reach the hotel fifteen minutes early and wait in my car. The hotel has a retro feel and is basically two long buildings flanking a crowded pool. I make it to the upstairs room right at eight and wait five minutes, feeling extremely self-conscious that everyone down at the pool is watching me. I'm wearing jeans, black gym shoes and a black t-shirt I bought here in town, making me stand out against all the families in bathing suits and shorts. There are several gay hotels in Palm Springs, but this is not one of them. Maybe they'll think I'm security.

I watch my phone until five after and knock twice on the door, opening it exactly thirty seconds later and locking it behind me. I step into a sparse living room with an orange sofa, wood table, TV and a dark archway which I assume leads to the bedroom. The only sound is the wall-unit air conditioner under the curtained window to my right. I hesitate, nervous, before stepping through the archway into the dimly lit bedroom.

As expected, I find two red envelopes on the bed. What I'm not prepared for is that these envelopes rest on the chest of a naked bodybuilder who is laying on his back, blindfolded, with his arms at his sides. I retrieve both envelopes, open number one, and read the unmarked card inside.

This is a piece of meat, a slave for you to use as you please. One rule: use condoms. One warning: he hates being spanked and is even stronger than he looks.

Enjoy your two hours,

Sir.

I set the card and the unopened envelope on the dresser and allow myself to inspect my prize. He has the body of a competitive bodybuilder but with a small tight waist rather than one of those bloated steroid guts. He has spiked red hair and a short-cropped beard, and his pale white skin is shaved smooth from his neck down. His nipples are dark pink and pronounced. His small lips and semi-hard cock are the same color as his nipples.

I scan the room—half-expecting I will find Liam sitting in a corner—before stepping forward. I'm very nervous, which I suppose makes it hotter, and my cock is doing its best to push its way out of my pants. I move to the side of the bed and drop to my knees in front of his head. He gasps when I trace my index finger across his Adam's apple and down his smooth, muscular neck. I continue down to the hard dimple between his upper pecs and he flexes to show off, tipping his head back and opening his mouth as if hungry for cock.

Not yet, stud.

I rub my hand down his chest and graze his pink little nipple, my touch causing him to writhe a little. He moans when

I touch the other nipple, so I cover his mouth with my free hand. This unknown stud licks and nibbles on my palm. His cock has become rock hard in a second. It's a little smaller than mine but looks great pushing against his abs like this.

I stand and take another look around the room to find lube, condoms, and bottles of water on a nightstand. I kick off my shoes, strip down to my white boxer briefs, and rub my cock through the cotton fabric while contemplating my situation. Who is this guy, and what—if anything—does he expect from me? Am I supposed to fuck him? I assume, by the condoms and lube, fucking him is on the table. Is this stranger my number five?

His mouth opens again as I step closer. I doubt he can see me through that blindfold, but I'm sure his other senses allow him to feel me move around the room. I look around again. We appear to be alone, but I would never see something like a hidden camera.

I'm paranoid, and ruining the moment.

Fuck it.

I reach under his arms and pull him toward me so that his head hangs off the edge of the bed. His mouth opens wide and he sticks his tongue out, clearly wanting. I figure two hours is plenty of time to have a little fun before giving him what he wants, so I straddle his head and squat down so that my ball sack smashes into his nose and mouth. This makes his cock dance. He reaches up to rub the back of my thighs, exposing his muscular and hairless pits.

He inhales and pulls me into him, sucking my balls through my briefs until they are drenched with spit. I squat down lower, straining his neck and crushing his face until he taps me on the thighs like a wrestler tapping out. I stand and allow him to catch his breath.

He's moving his head around as if searching for me through his blindfold, then opens his mouth again to let me know he's hungry. I peel my drenched briefs off, grab his bearded chin with one hand, and guide my cock down his throat with the other. I push, thrusting deeper and deeper until my cock is buried to the hilt and his prickly beard is poking the back of my balls. He isn't gagging at all but I can tell by his silent intensity he is unable to breathe with me so far down his throat. I hold this position while he begins to struggle, but I refuse to pull back until he finally taps out on my thigh.

The bodybuilder gasps, choking on his spit and probably a good deal of my pre-cum. Still, he clutches my thighs and pulls me in for more before I can ask how he is doing. I repeat the maneuver, over and over, pushing in so deep he can't breathe and making him hold it as long as he can until his taps on my thighs become desperate. He's out of breath after fifteen minutes, his massive chest muscles rippling as he gasps for air. Still grasping his chin for control, I drop to my knees and kiss his open mouth. He moans and begins twisting and writhing so much he's about to fall off the bed. I get in bed with him and pull him down so that he's no longer hanging off the edge.

Fuck; he's even heavier than he looks.

I climb on top of him so that our cocks press against each other. I kiss him again. He is more passionate than I would have imagined for a random hook-up, especially one who may not even know who I am or what I look like. My mind wanders to the thought Liam may have hired this guy for my pleasure. Is this guy an escort?

His hands roam up and down my body as though reading me by Braille as he grinds his dick against mine. I could do this all night and realize Liam gave me a two-hour time limit for this exact reason. I encourage him to turn on his side and twist around so that we are facing each other in a 69 position. I begin licking his dick clean of precum, guessing we are similar in height by the way our mouths align with our dicks. He is hungry for my dick and seems to get into it the most when I take control. I roll him onto his back and cram my shaft down his throat. I start blowing him as well but sense he is too close to shooting for this much stimulation, so I pull away. His dick tastes good and I wish I had more time to explore this muscle-beast. My hand finds his ass and I begin fingering his hole while I continue to fuck his face. His knees raise up as if on wires as soon as I touch his ass, amazing me.

His entire focus has shifted to his ass by the time I push my finger past the first knuckle. His smooth hole is hot and tight.

Pulling my dick out of his mouth, I twist around and move my hips between his legs so I can give his ass the attention it needs. I stretch awkwardly to reach the lube and condoms, thankful he can't how clumsy I am. I tear open the package with my teeth and stretch the condom over my aching cock, rolling it down to the shaft. I pour a little lube on my cock and strock it a few times until the condom shines in the dim hotel lighting.

He groans when I push against his hole. I push again, causing a sharp inhale of breath. He is tight: crazy tight. I apply lube to his ass and more to my cock and try again. He squeezes me with his huge thighs as I cram the head of my dick in his hole, making a low growling sound deep in his chest. I push a tiny bit further but he moans and gasps like I'm shoving a tree up his ass.

I stop and reassess.

Knowing he will never be able to take my dick in this state, I lube up his ass and begin working my index finger deep in his hot pink hole. Again, that deep growl in his chest. I push in my second finger, slowly, until the growling stops. He remains silent as I work my third finger in, so motionless I figure he is either deep in concentration or I've killed him.

I think he's ready.

I slowly pull my fingers away and stroke his cock a few times until he bats at my hand. I love the way he gasps when he hears me tear open another condom wrapper. "Show me that ass, boy," I growl, feeling ridiculous and realizing this is the first time either of us have said anything to each other. He turns over and arches his back, his smooth white ass glistening with lube.

I climb on top of him and reach under his neck with my right hand while positioning my cock with my left. A static jolt connects us as I make contact with his hole. He cries out as I push in without restraint, clutching my right forearm with both hands as though hanging on for life. I'm aware my dick is bigger than average but it's nothing crazy, making me wonder if he is actually in pain or just reacting for my benefit.

Fuck that. I push all the way in and hold the position, licking the back of his neck as I allow him to adjust. I remain locked deep inside of him for several minutes until he finally begins to relax his death-grip. Now I'm ready to seriously pound his ass into the bed.

He cries out again with his deep voice, so I muffle him with the palm of my hand. He chews on it but doesn't pull away. His ass feels amazing and I have to slow down several times to keep from shooting. I put my weight into it and drill into him as deep as I can. He bites me so hard at one point I fear my hand is bleeding but that just makes me pump harder. His moans change to choking gasps and he gets louder and more feral with every pump.

I become frenzied as I tear into his hole until my balls pull up tight and begin to burn. I pull out at the last minute, tear off the condom and shoot my load all over his bulging back and ass until I am gasping as hard as he.

I work to catch my breath while massaging his hard ass. He flexes at my touch, probably showing off. Whatever his motivation, he looks amazing. Lifting myself from him, I turn him over on his back only to find a massive pool of cum all over the sheets: he must have shot his wad while I was fucking him.

"Wow," is the most succinct thing I can think of saying.

"Thank you," are the first two words I've ever heard him say. He has a deep voice with a strong southern accent.

I lean in and kiss him. "Mind if I use the shower?"

He shakes his head, still blindfolded, and smiles. Every muscle on his body flexes as he stretches like a cat. I grab the lube and squeeze some on his belly, rubbing it over his torso until he shines.

"Want to join me in the shower?"

Again, he shakes his head and smiles.

I stumble into the bathroom as though drunk and quickly rinse off. I return to find him lying spread eagle on his back, glistening with lube just as I left him. I stand in the bathroom doorway and enjoy the view for a few minutes. The clock by the bed claims it is nine forty-seven.

Damn, those two hours went by quickly.

I get dressed before leaning down to kiss him again. "Gonna lay there in our jizz all night, you hot fuck?"

He laughs and cuddles into the bed like a puppy. I'm tempted to take a photo of his amazing body but figure that is just creepy.

I pick up the second envelope from the dresser and read the card which states there is a gift for me in the top right drawer I am not permitted to use tonight. I open the drawer and find the black leather paddle I used on Rik's ass a few weeks ago. I give it a slow sniff before letting myself out, wondering what the crowd at the pool must think of my walking down the stairs with a paddle in my hand.

Let them think what they want.

I get in the car, crank on the air conditioner, and call Liam.

"Have fun?"

"That was amazing. Thank you for the paddle, Sir: I love it"

"You kissed him."

"Hell yeah. He is so fucking sexy.

Liam sighs. "Oh, honey."

"Were you watching?"

Liam laughs. "He texted me."

"Was kissing him against the rules?"

"No, but … it wasn't a date. He was meat. Do you kiss meat?"

"I do when it's fillet mignon."

He chuckles. "I said you were allowed to do whatever you wanted, so that's fine. He just doesn't like kissing."

"He seemed to like it. Love it, even."

"Okay," Liam says after a pause. "Have a great night, sweet boy."

CHAPTER SIX

I've been referring to Liam as "Sir" this past month and while I still don't understand the dynamics of our relationship, it just seems to fit. Liam and Rik are amazing men and while Rik is always an active part of the conversation, Liam has subtly taken over the role as my mentor, instructor, confidant, and friend. There's something about receiving fatherly advice from someone who isn't my father I find myself embracing. I know if I explained the situation to anyone, they would think it creepy. Rik is crazy-flirty and I'd love to have sex with him again if he's game. Liam, however, has never made a sexual move on me; not even in a joking way. He doesn't appear to have any plans for me, no predetermined goals, and has become the perfect guide in so many aspects of life. I haven't seen either of them these past two weeks because they have been in New Orleans for work. I've learned they own boutique hotels in cities such as New Orleans, Denver, Portland and Seattle.

I'm sitting on my bed, wrapping Liam's birthday present. I had no idea what to get someone who can buy whatever he wants, so I settled on a black leather frame I found at a little store in Palm Desert. I added a photo of the three of us taken at a restaurant a few weeks ago. They invited me to join them tonight at their home for a dinner party and while Rik assured me it will be small and casual, I am nervous. My idea of a big birthday party is having my Italian aunts bring all their kids over for pasta and poker. I'm not comfortable in formal social situations and am worried Rik's idea of casual will be over-the-top. I don't want to embarrass them in front of their friends.

I have an hour before the party, so I shower and change

into my black jeans and a black polo shirt. I bought the shirt this afternoon and it may be too tight; more appropriate for a nightclub than a dinner party at a mansion. I look at myself in the mirror as I try to tame my hair with molding clay: not to be cocky, but I look pretty good today. I've added more muscle to my chest and shoulders yet have lost an inch from my waist. I kind of look like a different person because I have become ridiculously tan, looking more Italian than Norwegian. The black leather boots I also bought today make me two inches taller.

I park in their huge circular driveway right on time and let myself in, still amazed by the enormity of their house. Rik once mentioned there are six bedrooms, but then he said eight another day. I walk through the foyer and under the giant black staircase into the dining room, where Liam greets me with a hug. He's wearing dark-grey jeans and a black polo shirt with a navy-blue collar. His hair and beard are newly-trimmed and his green eyes sparkle in the light of the candles stretching down the long black table. There are only four place settings.

"Happy birthday, Sir." I hand him his gift.

"Thank you, Caine." He sets the gift on the table and rubs the smooth cloth of my shirt. "You look nice tonight."

I nod in gratitude and follow him through what I call the game room due to the pool table and out to their patio bar. The pool and expansive yard glow with hundreds of hanging lights which sway in the cool breeze. It has been in the 90s all week but tonight is perfect.

Liam assumes position at the bar like the captain of a ship. "Gin and tonic?"

"It's your birthday; what are you drinking?"

Liam retrieves two martini glasses and fills them with ice and water. "Eiko martinis, then."

I've never heard of Eiko, but nod just the same.

"Japanese vodka," he says. "Very subtle. You'll love it."

I glance around the empty yard as he makes our drinks. "Am I early?"

Liam asks if I want a lemon or an olive but drops a lemon

peel in both glasses before I can respond. He hands me the drink and raises his glass with another wink. "It's just the four of us tonight."

I try hiding the surprise from my face and sip the martini. He's right, as usual; I love it. By four of us I assume he means Rik and Aiden, but I never know what to expect with Sir. Liam describes Aiden as their son or boy, depending on their mood at the time. I have a hundred questions about that but feel weird prying into their personal and sexual lives. I've yet to meet him but know he lives somewhere in the house. I always assumed Aiden was the slave they mentioned, but they assured me that is another individual who comes over every Sunday.

"Rik and Aiden are getting dinner ready."

"I thought you said, uh...,"

"Don't worry, Rik isn't cooking. Aiden's actually a great cook, but we ordered dinner from Miro's. Dinner was delivered a few minutes before you arrived."

As if on cue, Rik joins us and stretches up to kiss my cheek. "If you get any darker, we can tell people you are my Cuban brother." He walks around the bar and hugs Liam. "Your birthday feast is ready."

I take my drink and follow them back to the dining room, stopping short when I see who is placing a tray of meat on the table.

Liam rubs my arm. "Surprise."

The boy in front of me is the blindfolded bodybuilder I had so much fun with three weeks ago.

I think I gasp. "I didn't realize. You never told me."

"Where's the fun in that?"

"Liam loves surprises," Rik says. "You'll get used to it."

The boy turns to me with an outstretched hand. "Nice to finally see you. I'm Aiden."

I shake his offered hand and laugh.

Aiden gives a crooked smirk and a shrug of his muscular shoulders. He's wearing sandals, tan shorts, and a baggy powder-blue t-shirt which makes his pale blue eyes glow. His red hair is

41

cropped short on the sides and spiked high on top. His beard is a little scruffier than when I first saw him. He looks like a Viking superhero.

"You're right, Sir," Aiden says in a deep southern drawl as he continues looking at me.

"Naturally," Liam responds.

Aiden continues staring at me without pretense. Fair enough, I figure, as I can't pull away from his eyes. Another smirk before he turns back to the table.

"Sit here by me." Liam indicates a chair in the center of the table. Rik reappears from the kitchen with more food and sits across from Liam. Aiden joins us a few seconds later and sits across from me.

Rik pours champagne for Liam, Aiden and myself. I realize, finally, I've never Rik drink anything but water or iced tea. He raises his glass of water, still standing. "Here's to another amazing year, my love."

The four of us raise our glasses and wish Liam a happy birthday.

"This is all from Miro's, a local steakhouse with a Yugoslavian flare," Rik says to me. "Look here, we have red cabbage salad, crab cakes which are Liam's favorite." Rik is pointing to each dish as he describes them. "Beef stroganoff, branzino which is a type of sea bass, two orders of Jidori chicken because Aiden will eat an entire portion himself, T-bone, and lamb chops."

I look at the meal in awe. "There's enough for eight of us."

"Ha," Liam adds. "He hasn't seen Aiden eat."

Oh, I've seen him eat, I remember with a grin. I am so proud of myself for not saying it out loud. I learn Aiden is twenty-two, has competed in two bodybuilding competitions, and works as a personal trainer at a small gym here in Palm Springs.

"Aiden's the most popular trainer in the desert, "Rik says. "All the gays love the idea of having such a sexy straight trainer."

"You're straight?"

Aiden simply shrugs and continues eating.

I must look confused because Liam starts laughing and pats

my arm. "You'll drive yourself crazy trying to figure this one out. Hell, he hasn't figured himself out."

I ask Aiden how they met but Liam answers. "We were in New Orleans for several months in 2015 while launching the hotel. We hired Aiden one night for a muscle-worship session."

"Several nights," Rik adds.

"Aiden was, what, nineteen at the time?"

Aiden nods.

I have to ask. "What exactly does a muscle-worship session entail?"

"You know," Aiden answers, "Striping, flexing and whatever. It was different with each client."

"We were immediately impressed by his confidence, but his cocky playfulness couldn't hide his pain." Liam turns to me. "His family kicked him out at fifteen and he had been living on the streets of New Orleans, turning tricks to survive."

"It wasn't so bad." Aiden leans in for more chicken. "I spent the days at the gym where I had access to a bathroom and shower, and I would often be invited to spend the nights with whomever hired me."

"You had sex with them?"

Aiden nods.

"All men?"

"Mostly men, but some women. Probably 90% men."

"And you're straight."

His shrug kills me. "Does it matter? I like sex. Sex comes easy for me and people enjoy me. You enjoyed me."

I think Rik picks up on my discomfort because he jumps into the conversation. "Aiden was so sweet, but so sad. He was HIV positive and addicted to meth by the time he was sixteen. His beautiful eyes were empty, you can't imagine."

"I wasn't addicted, it just helped me stay awake when I had nowhere to sleep."

Rik rolls his eyes. "I told Liam we had to rescue him."

"He wasn't a puppy," Liam scolded.

"Wasn't he?"

"He moved here with us and Rik cleaned him up."

"Yes," Rik agrees. "We added him to our medical insurance and got him on antiviral meds, then helped him complete high school. Within a year he had grown into a completely different person. He wanted to work in a gym—no surprise to anyone—and became a certified personal trainer."

"I'm their charity case."

Rik hushed him. "You deserve to be happy."

I am amazed once again at their level of candor. No subject is taboo in this house. The meal is amazing, and I try a little of everything as they chat about the hotel they are opening in Key West.

Liam pours more champagne as Rik and Aiden clear the table. "Don't be uncomfortable around Aiden. I think he likes you, but don't let yourself fall for him."

"He's really straight?"

Liam sighs. "I know it's much easier to say than practice, but try not to get hung up on labels like straight or gay, top or bottom, masculine or feminine. We are rarely black or white on such things and most of us are floating somewhere between the extremes. Where do you float?"

"I'm pretty sure I'm 100% gay. I mean, I've had sex with a girl in high school but …, didn't we all?"

"Rik has never had sex with a woman, but I'm sure he would in the right situation. I was married to a woman but that's another story for another night. Aiden will have sex with anyone, but he's an exhibitionist and loves showing off. That's his fetish; exhibitionism. He feeds off the adoration of others. That's why he had so much fun with you that night."

"Oh?"

Liam chuckles. "You worry he was faking it."

"I guess, maybe."

"He loved it. He said he could taste your energy. He likes pleasing people. Unfortunately, his life experiences have caused him to believe the only way he can please people is with his body. Why do you think he works so hard at perfecting it?"

"That's horrible."

"Stop." Liam rubs my thigh. "I know that look. Don't feel guilty for enjoying him. Aiden is a bright young man and he'll learn to value himself over time. We encourage him onto other paths toward self-worth and self-confidence. You and Aiden are more similar than you may realize."

"I'm shy."

"Because you have shame, but of what?"

"Uh …,"

"I don't expect you to answer me, but I want you to keep that question in mind as you progress."

"Progress?"

"With your fetish of choice."

"And what would that be?"

Liam smiles. "Bondage and domination, it is written all over you. "I'm going to train you to be a bondage master in order to work past your shame."

I'm incredulous and can't muster a response. Luckily, Rik and Aiden return with four cupcakes lit with sparkling candles. We sing happy birthday and Liam blows the candles out with one big puff."

"What did you wish for, Sir?" Aiden asks.

Liam winks at me. "It's a surprise."

Rik is watching Aiden pretend to eat his cupcake. "Yours is sugar-free."

Aiden nods in appreciation and takes a tiny bite. I restrain my sudden need to lean across the table and lick the white frosting from his lips. "Diabetic?"

Aiden shakes his head.

Rik laughs. "Caine is waiting for an explanation, yes?"

"Aiden is many things," Liam says, "but forthcoming isn't one of them."

Aiden looks at me like he is just realizing we are talking about him. "I'll tell you anything."

Liam taps me with his elbow. "If you ask."

Aiden shrugs and takes another small bite.

Liam stands from the table. "I say we open another bottle of champagne and move this little party to the jacuzzi."

"It's your birthday," Rik salutes with his water glass. "We can move our little party to Paris if you wish."

"Can I borrow a bathing suit?"

"No!" Rik yells, then laughs. "Bathing suits are not allowed in this house. Ever."

"We have very few house rules, but this is one of them," Liam says with a smile. "Besides, someone with your body should be naked as much as possible."

Rik nods. "If I had your dick, I would never wear clothes."

"Rik, my love, you've had his dick. Both of you trouble-makers have."

Aiden gives a crooked grin, stands, and pulls his shirt off. I enjoy watching him carefully fold his shirt before he sets it on the table. His shorts are next. He isn't wearing underwear and his hard dick presses up against his muscular abs.

Liam laughs. "You get used to that after a while."

"A light breeze is all it takes to set this one off." Rik wraps his hand around Aiden's dick and guides him around the table and out the back. "Come with me, son."

Liam indicates we follow. "We are rather inappropriate parents."

I laugh and begin to feel a little less uncomfortable. I'm not sure what they have planned but, for some reason, I doubt it will be sexual: something about Liam's calm demeaner triggers a question I have been sitting on all night. "Sir?"

Liam turns to me.

"Tonight has been great and I mean no disrespect, but ..."

"What?"

"I expected something bigger for your birthday."

Liam nods as we continue through the patio lounge into the yard. "Our life is grand and we have been crazy-busy launching a new hotel every-other year. Our professional life is filled with pomp and uncomfortable formal parties. I prefer celebrating my birthday in peace with my family."

I watch Liam pull another bottle of champagne from the patio refrigerator and follow him to the pool. Rik is naked and standing on a table between two lounge chairs, swaying his small hips to music unheard. The breeze-touched trees cause lights to flicker and dance off his tightly-muscled torso. Rik turns and juts his ass at us. "Come and get it."

"Insanity," I mumble in appreciation.

Aiden appears from around a tree and wraps his huge arms around Rik's thighs. Lifting him from the table without effort, Aiden tosses Rik into the pool. Liam takes my hand and guides me to the pool. "Let's join the insanity, or we can just relax in the jacuzzi and watch these clowns; you can do whatever you want."

"And yes," Liam answers my unasked question. "You are part of this crazy family."

CHAPTER SEVEN

I wake with the sun to find three pairs of eyes staring at me. I let the dogs sleep with me last night because Mitch and Stefani are out of town. The little dogs have taken over the queen-sized bed.

I stand, stretch, and pull on a pair of underwear. My body aches from the past three days of twelve-hour shifts in the busy ICU. This hospital is a little smaller than Albuquerque Presbyterian, but their ICU is busier than I'm used to. I thought this contract would be easier because California only allows an ICU nurse to care for two patients at a time, but there is less support here and no one is ever available to assist me. Turning my four-hundred pound patient by myself even two hours wore me out.

The dogs prance in and out of the door I left open for them. "Who wants breakfast?" The three of them—Vinnie in particular —go insane as though they are starving. They circle around me as I shuffle across the yard and feed them in the main house. I return to the back yard and admire how the San Jacinto mountains glow with the sunrise. It's not even six and its already hot.

One of Mitch's speedos hangs over the back of a patio chair, this one yellow with thick black stripes. My cock warms with the thought there is probably a drawer filled with various speedos somewhere in their bedroom. I look around the yard as though being watched before running the back of my fingers across the yellow and black nylon. I rub the smooth material between my finger and thumb, imagining it stretched tight over Mitch's impressive bulge. I slowly lift the speedo and press it against my face, inhaling what I imagined would be the scent of his manliness. Instead, the speedo smells of pool water. That doesn't stop my cock from throbbing, though.

I look around the yard again and catch the judging eye of Vinnie watching me through the glass door. "Vin, go inside," I whisper, which only makes the other two dogs appear. I pull my underwear off and rub the speedo against my hardening cock. I continue rubbing against it, imagining the fabric stretched out across Mitch's ass, until it is wet with pre-cum. I bend over and draw the speedo up one leg and then the other, struggling a bit to pull it over my ass because Mitch's waist is smaller than mine. Pushing my cock down to conceal it under the fabric, I admire Mitch's speedos in my muted reflection in the glass door. I rub the fabric for a few minutes until my cock is fighting to escape the confines of this small bathing suit.

I should cum in them, right here in front of the trio of Italian Greyhounds, and mark it as mine.

Instead, I jump in the pool with a loud splash and swim several laps until my mind and cock are somewhat at ease. I float on my back and admire the mountains. There is a beautiful sensuality to Palm Springs, in the energy radiating from every stone or stretch of sand, in the rustling hum of palm trees dancing in the warm breeze. The weather and the smell of the wind is nothing like Albuquerque. It hits me, all at once, that I don't miss home at all. I'm in week eight of my thirteen-week contract here. I don't know where I will go next, but I know I will miss the desert when I leave.

I remain in the pool for what feels like hours until my need for coffee overwhelms my need for physical contact with Mitch and his pool. I shower and shave, get dressed, and cover my messy mop of hair with a ballcap. I drive through the neighborhood of mid-century modern homes and turn left on North Palm Canyon Drive to reach my favorite coffee shop. It is one of the numerous gay-owned Palm Springs businesses but, like most places here, is filled with retired straight couples. I walk through the little downtown area with my iced americano as I do on most of my days off, admiring the unique restaurants and art galleries which line the one-way boulevard. I cross the street at the fancy hotel which opened earlier this year and work my way back to my car.

I get home and decide reading out in the sun is about as much effort as I want to give on my first of three days off. I'm tempted to put the speedo back on but opt for my own board shorts. I pour myself into a lounge chair and begin reading a new book on my phone when I am interrupted by a text from Aiden.

What are you doing today?

Staying near the pool, I type back. *It's too hot for anything else.*

Let's escape this heat together. I have one more client here at the gym and can be at your place by noon.

The thought of spending the day with Aiden makes me glad I didn't jack off this morning. *Sounds good, see you then.*

Aiden arrives wearing his typical sleeveless flannel shirt, baggy cargo shorts and gym shoes. His shoes and shirt are lime green today.

"Your sneakers always match the color of your shirt," I comment as a greeting. "How many pair do you own?"

"Not that many." He gives me a hard hug, squeezing my ribs.

"Ugh," I squeak in jest. I haven't figured if he hugs so hard to show off or if he is unaware of his strength, but it is something I have learned to brace myself for.

Aiden glances at my bare feet. "Put on shoes; we're going hiking."

"In this heat?"

"Trust me."

Aiden drives us in his navy-blue pick-up to the Palm Springs Aerial Tramway. There's a line out the door of the base station but he assures me this is nothing compared to a weekend and that we won't have to wait long.

"I can't believe you haven't checked this out yet," Aiden says in his smooth Louisiana drawl as we wait in line for the tram. "You've been here, what, two months?"

I nod.

"What do you do on your days off other than workout at the wrong gym and tan?"

Aiden has been trying to convince me to leave World Gym and work out with him, but he'd be too big a distraction for me to get any serious lifting done around him. "Catch up on the sleep I am deprived during the days I work. Read."

Aiden taps my forehead. "Don't get too smart for me."

"That's unlikely."

"Pshh," Aiden whistles through his teeth. "You don't fool me. Nursing school is hard. You work in ICU and deal with all sorts of shit I can't imagine."

"I've seen things."

"I could never do it. My brain isn't built like that."

"I'm sure you can do anything you set your mind to."

Aiden leans forward with an unexpected kiss on my mouth, igniting a giddy tingle that races down my body to rest in my balls. I must be showing my surprise because he smiles and straightens my hat. To say Aiden is beautiful is a lesson in understatement, as I find myself falling for him every time his pale eyes lock onto mine. I mean, the pretty eyes, flawless skin and crazy muscles would turn anyone's head. It's more than that, though: He resonates a gentle charisma I am drawn into. Everyone should be blessed with an Aiden.

"I haven't even seen the ocean since I've been here."

Aiden looks incredulous. "You've never seen the ocean?"

"As a kid. My parents took me to Disneyland when I was thirteen. We stayed at some hotel in Newport Beach."

"San Diego and Orange County are only ninety-minues away. Are you working tomorrow?"

I shake my head, enjoying his excitement.

"I'm taking you to the beach. Huntington Beach is my favorite, but maybe we can drive up to Muscle Beach in Venice."

"Sounds great."

We file into what I keep being told is the world's largest rotating aerial tram car and ascend the two-and-a-half-mile journey in roughly ten minutes. I get the point of this excursion as soon as I step out of the upper tram station and follow Aiden to a crowded observation deck.

"It has to be thirty degrees cooler up here," I say, looking out at the expanse of Coachella Valley before and below us.

"More like forty." Aiden points to a large thermometer on the wall behind us. "It's sixty-four degrees up here and it's supposed to be one hundred and five in town today."

We spend a few hours walking along the pine-scented trails and have lunch at one of the restaurants before heading back down into the desert heat. Aiden returns me to Mitch and Stephani's house, then surprises me when he follows me in. "What are you doing the rest of the night?"

"Nothing much: swim, drink beer, and watch TV. Mitch and Stefani won't be back until tomorrow night."

"That sounds perfect." Aiden jogs in front of me, hops out of his shorts while unsnapping his shirt (I had no idea it snapped, that can be fun), pulls off his shoes and dives naked into the pool.

I shake my head in wonder and join him, tearing my clothes off and tossing them behind me. I dive deep into the warm water and emerge next to him. Aiden turns to me with a cocky grin, his eyes the color of pool water. I make the mistake of initiating an underwater wrestling match until he locks me in a choke hold and nearly drowns me. He apologizes as I cough out a gallon of salt water. "You had some good moves so I figured I had to lock you out fast before you took me down."

I laugh and cough. "It's cool but, … fuck, you are strong." I pull myself out of the pool and catch my breath. The sky is a clear, deep blue and there's a slight breeze. I could lay here on my back all day if the concrete wasn't so hot, so I plop down in a lounge chair in defeat. "You win that one. And here I thought all those muscles were just for show."

Aiden lifts a wooden lounge over his head and positions it next to me, then lowers himself into it with a sigh. He flexes his bicep with a smile. "They are for show; for showing off."

"Jesus," I groan. I watch him relax and settle into the lounge. "Why bodybuilding?"

"I like lifting."

I'm about to drop the subject but remember Liam

explaining how Aiden needs to be pushed. "Tell me more."

Aiden turns on his side and props his head up with his hand. "My brothers set up a gym in our carport. They are way older than me, and working out with them was one of the only ways I could connect with them.

What was it like?

Aiden smiles. "Is this the part where I tell you the story of my life?"

I nod.

He clears his throat. "I was born a poor yet proud farmer," he begins in a silly cowboy accent.

"No, for real."

"You're no fun," he drawls in his real voice. "Fine. I was born in Baton Rouge, the youngest of three boys. My mother died of tuberculosis when I was four, so I really don't remember her."

"Oh, shit."

"I'm told she was sweet as honey and pretty like a sunset. They say I have her eyes but I got my red hair from my Irish Daddy. You may have guessed the Irish part from my last name.

"I have no idea what you last name is."

"Hmm."

"What, that surprises you?"

"Just that most guys who hook up with me tend to look me up on the internet and claim to know everything about me."

"I've been busy," I say with a smile.

"Anyway, Daddy was in construction. After my brothers moved out in 2008, he moved the two of us to New Orleans because there was more work there due to Katrina. Daddy set up a gym on our porch with my brothers' old equipment and used to work out with me. I was the most muscular kid in Desire."

"Desire?"

"A shitty little neighborhood in New Orleans. Daddy worked long hours but the neighbors were nice to me. Too nice. I was around fifteen when Daddy caught me blowing the neighbor, a guy at least thirty years older. Daddy beat the fuck outta that man before pointing his nine-millimeter in my face. He told me he would shoot me dead if he ever saw me again."

I sit up. "Jesus!"

"I knew he meant it, the way you just know things. Then I did some stupid shit you already heard about for a few years before Liam and Rik found me."

"Wow. Do you miss it?

"Letting people fuck me for money?"

"No, I meant—"

"Calm down, boy: I know what you meant. I don't miss New Orleans. It wasn't all bad, though. You should check it out sometime."

"With you as my tour guide?"

"Mmm hmm," he groans with a nod.

I guess that's all he's going to say on the subject because he rolls onto his back, covers his eyes with his hands, and appears to fall asleep. His muscles bounce and ripple with each breath and his pale smooth skin beads with pool water. He turns toward me and watches me watch him. Normally, I would look away in embarrassment but I force myself to hold gentle eye contact.

We look into each other for several minutes before he stands without a word and walks into my place. I follow him inside the air-conditioned room and close the door behind us.

"You drive me crazy," I say before I can stop myself.

Aiden gives me his crooked smile. "Then do something about it."

I gently wrap my hand around the back of his thick neck and push my lips against his, allowing him time to pull away if he chooses. Aiden parts his lips and leans into me, cupping my bare ass with his hands. The connection is intense and immediate —one of those tricks of chemistry that can never be faked—and I know he feels it as well. I clutch his arms as he pulls me closer to him until his hard cock is pressing against mine.

He pulls his mouth away and says "you make me horny" with a soft moan. His clear pale eyes look deep into me. He cocks his head to the left and looks like he's trying to figure me out.

"What?"

Aiden grips my ass and lifts me up so high I nearly hit the ceiling fan. I cling to his neck as he carries me to the bed and topples down on me with a thud. His elbows catch the brunt of our weight but I still let out an involuntary grunt. "You'll crush me if you're not careful," I say as I run my fingers through his wet hair.

"Naw."

I'm losing myself as Aiden rubs his dick against mine. I try pushing him to the side but he is locked in position. I try again, harder, but he doesn't budge. I remain pinned under his weight and allow him to have his fun for a while before trying to push him away again. "Grr. I want to switch places."

Aiden smiles with mischief and rolls over on his back next to me. "You can do whatever you want."

I straddle him and brush his red hair from his eyes. Grabbing both his wrists, I spread his arms out and above his head and push them into the bed with my weight. He's squirming around and acting like he can't break free even though I know he can toss me through the window if he chooses.

"Where are you hiding the chains?"

"I don't know about chains, but Liam signed me up for a rope-play class later this month."

Aiden cranes his neck and kisses me. "Of course he did, Liam junior."

I lightly chew his lower lip before tracing my tongue down his muscular neck. I take my time tasting his neck, his shoulder, his chest. His skin is soft and smells of salt water and cinnamon. He inhales sharply as soon as I reach his left nipple. I feel his cock throbbing against my chest, so I continue teasing him as he pretends to try and wrestle his way free. He eventually gives up his struggle with an exaggerated sigh.

I bite his nipple, igniting a spasm throughout his body. "Damn."

"You clearly hate that."

"I love it, but I want to touch you."

I let go of his wrists and suck on his nipple, grinding my teeth against it.

Aiden grips my head with both hands but doesn't pull me away. "Shit, boy" he hisses. "This body is all for show, remember? Be gentle."

I take his left hand and lightly guide it behind his neck, admiring the way his lat muscles flare out like a wing. I lick his shaven underarm, noting only a light hint of stubble which makes me think he's not very hairy to begin with. He's not wearing deodorant and while he doesn't stink, he certainly smells and tastes like a man. I begin chewing on his pit, making him squirm.

"Hey!" he yells. He's pretending he doesn't like it, but I can feel his cock pulsating. He wraps his legs around my torso and rolls me over and under him with surprising strength.

"Dang," I gasp. "Did you wrestle as a kid?"

"Only when they paid me to."

I groan and try to wiggle away. He pins me down until I give up with a laugh.

He continues staring down at me.

"What?"

"You're fun to watch."

I shake my head. "I'm sure there's something in here I can use as a blindfold."

"Naw." He gives a smirk and slides down my body until his face hovers over my cock. He licks the underside of the shaft, causing my cock to bounce, then wraps his lips around the head and swallows me until his beard presses into my balls.

"Holy fuck," I moan as my eyes roll back and my hands wrap around his skull. His mouth is electric and his moans drive me insane as he chokes and gags. I attempt to slow his rhythm but he ignores me, continuing to work my bone like it's a competition until I am gasping. I resist my building need to skull-fuck a load down his throat by grabbing his hair and guiding him up my body until his mouth reconnects with mine. He kisses me with hunger as he rubs his ass against my cock.

He glances at my nightstand. My smile makes him laugh as I twist over and hand him condoms, lube and a towel. I rub his hard chest and marvel at the excitement in his eyes as he pulls a condom over my cock and lubes it up like a pro. He leans forward and kisses me again while reaching back and guiding my cock toward his ass. His face twitches when we make contact. He pushes against me, shuddering with the pressure, and gasps when my head pushes into his vice of an ass. Sweat beads on his forehead. "Start slow, big boy."

I hold back from thrusting deep inside him and allow Aiden to slowly work his way down my shaft until my balls are pressing against his quivering ass cheeks. Only after his pained expression melts into a wink of confidence do I begin slowly pumping his hole. He takes each thrust with a soft grunt, his hands clutching my pecs and his eyes locked to mine. I grip his ass as though I am going to tear it in two and force myself deep inside him with each thrust.

His eyes go wild and he tries to pull himself away from me. "Caine, stop! You're gonna make me spunk."

I stop moving and enjoy his look of concentration. "Not yet," I say, rolling him over on his back without breaking our connection. I maneuver onto my knees so that his huge legs are wrapped around my waist as I take a moment to appreciate the view. Aiden's pink dick is pressed against his hairless body, oozing with precum. I wrap my hand around it and pull it towards me until he gasps, clutching it as I continue fucking him. I stop when he gets close to shooting, allowing him to catch his breath before resuming my attack on his ass. I bring him close, over and over, until he begins beating my chest with his fists.

"I can't take any more," he pleads. "You're killing me with that monster."

I'm in love with the desperation in his voice and the fire in his eyes. I want to prolong this moment as long as possible, though the thought of setting this boy off is excruciating. I pull on his cock and pound his ass until his legs tighten around me and his mouth opens wide in a silent scream. His entire body tenses as he shoots a sudden, massive load all over his chest and abs. I do my best not to shoot as his rigid muscles relax one by one and his silence is finally broken by a desperate gasp.

I watch in awe as he slowly comes back from wherever his intense orgasm had taken him and a look of awareness returns to his eyes. "Damn," is all I can think of saying, making him chuckle. I use the towel to wipe up his load which is pooling between the hard ridges of his abs and slowly, slowly pull out of him. I want nothing more than to roll him over and continue fucking his beautiful ass, but decide to let him rest a few minutes. I pull the condom off and toss it on the floor behind me, roll Aiden on his side, and wrap myself around him. He pushes into me with a sigh and moans with pleasure as I trace my fingertips along his broad shoulder and neck.

"Cullen," he mumbles.

I glance at him.

"My last name is Cullen."

"Pleased to meet you, mister Cullen."

His chest shakes with a chuckle as he presses his ass against me. "I want more," he says with a raspy drawl.

"Damn right."

Aiden pulls my arm around him and is lightly snoring within minutes. I allow him to continue sleeping for thirty minutes or so until the sensation of my throbbing cock against his muscular ass begins driving me insane. I lick the back of his neck and chew on his ear until he finally turns toward me with a smile. "You let me fall asleep."

"Just a little."

"I'm sorry. Why didn't you wake me?

I want to tell him how much I love watching him sleep, having his muscled body against me in bed like this, and that I would happily lie here and watch him sleep all night. Instead, I say "I wanted you to build up enough energy for round two."

He reaches between us and squeezes my cock. "Feels like you have enough energy for both of us."

I playfully grab a handful of his hair and pull his head back so that I can kiss his neck. I twist around and roll him over on his back so that I can continue tracing my tongue across his chest and down his stomach. I continue past his belly button to find his twenty-two-year-old dick rock hard and bouncing with his heartbeat.

"Doesn't take long to recharge."

"I'm on a light cycle of testosterone and trenbolone. It makes me super horny."

"Wow."

"I'm serious. I have to jack off three times a night just to fall asleep.

"I'd like to watch that sometime."

"Yes yes yes," He says with a laugh.

I lick the salty bead of precum from the tip of his cock. This sets him off: he clutches my head and pushes his cock against my mouth, then hesitates.

I pat his chest. "You can be as rough as you want. I won't break." I open my mouth and teasingly lick the base of his cock head until he pushes it deep down my throat. Reaching under him, I roll us around so that I'm flat on my back with him on top of me. He puts his weight into it and pushes so far down my throat I am unable to breath, his body trembling with the strain. I grasp his hips and am about to tap out when he pulls back enough on his own, as if knowing exactly how long I can hold my breath.

Aiden repeats this maneuver over and over, holding me down each time until I am unable to breath before releasing me to gasp for a quick breath. He pushes back in and starts fucking my throat, growing more and more violent with every thrust. He's making an amazing sound—something between a gasp and a sob —and I stroke my aching cock and prepare to swallow his load.

He stops at what I assume is the brink of his orgasm, giving me a chance to enjoy the sensation of his cock pulsing against my tongue, before resuming his attack on my mouth. His legs tremble as he power-fucks my throat for a few minutes until he forces himself to pull away from me.

"I almost shot," he gasps, rolling over on his back.

My throat aches and I suspect my lips are bruised, but I keep these observations to myself as I twist back around and climb on top of him. Aiden wraps his hands around the back of my head and we kiss, deep and long. This chemistry between us is amazing and I find myself unable to stop dwelling on the fact he claims to be straight.

Maybe it has nothing to do with me. Maybe it's just the steroids.

Fuck.

I pull away from the kiss and hover above him. His eyes look cloudy in this near-sunset light.

"What?" he asks with a grin.

I can't think of a way to make "I'm doing my best not to fall in love with you" not sound creepy. "Roll over," I say with a nudge.

Aiden rolls onto his stomach and rocks back and forth, teasing me with his hard ass. "I get a massage?"

I run my fingers from his neck down to his butt, creating goose-bumps on his smooth, flawless skin. "Something like that." I straddle him and begin kneading his shoulders, which have light freckles I hadn't noticed before. He relaxes for a few minutes as I work his tight muscles, then arches his back and moves down a few inches so that his ass is pushing against my hard cock. "Now you're in trouble."

He reaches across to the night stand and tosses a few condoms and the bottle of lube at me. "Don't I know it."

Leaning forward, I wrap my hand around the front of his neck and gentle pull him up from the pillow, twisting his head so we can kiss. He seems to melt in my arms as I lose myself in the passion of the kiss until my cock seems to find his ass all on its own. He drops back down in the pillow and pushes his ass against me, teasing me … daring me. I pat his ass, remembering Liam's warning about not spanking him, and pull him back so that he is on his knees with his ass in the air. I drizzle lube down his smooth crack and press my thumb against his hole. Wiggling my thumb, I eventually break the seal.

"Be gentle, boy. My butt is still sore from you fucking it."

I sit back and admire his ass as I roll a condom over my dick. His shaved balls hang low between his thighs and are swaying with the rhythm of him jacking off. I grab his hip in one hand and pull him towards me, rubbing my dick against the lube on his ass a few times before pushing inside him.

"Shit!" he yells playfully as he tries to pull away. "You call that gentle?"

There's nothing gentle about this muscled monster. I respond with another pat on his ass as I push further inside him. Grasping his hips with both hands, I hold this position until his tension eases and he stops pulling away. I pull my dick nearly all the way out and then slowly back, enjoying the way it makes the muscles in his back and shoulders flex. Out and back, over and over, just like we did that time he was blindfolded in that motel room. Aiden is jacking off with a frenzy and his back is shiny with sweat. I release his hips and rub the sweat from his back as he rocks his ass back and forth on my cock. He grows silent and his hole clamps onto me.

"I'm not stopping if you shoot," I say too late, as I can feel the constrictions of his orgasm clenching around my dick.

"Fuck," he moans, sounding both guilty and relieved. "I shot all over your sheets."

His moan makes me laugh. "There's a washing machine." I push him down onto his load and continue pounding his ass. He grunts like an animal and I can't tell if he loves it or hates it, but he's not telling me to stop. I press him down under my weight, wrap my arms around his chest, and fuck the hell out of him until I am trembling with the need for release. The tension reaches critical mass and I pull out and tear the condom off at the last possible moment. "Fuck, fuck, fuck!" I shout, sending a silent apology to the neighbors as I shoot my load all over his back and ass.

"Holy fuck," I gasp, unable to control my convulsing body as I ride out my orgasm. My ears ring and my skin hums as I slowly descend this high. Allowing my weight to drop back down on him, I gently kiss the back of his neck. "Fuck," I whisper in his ear. I grab the towel and wipe up what I can before rolling over on my back with what I am sure is a big goofy smile. I pull him towards me, out of his pool of jizz.

"*C'était super,*" he says, reminding me he's from Louisiana.

I lean over and kiss his face. "Is that a good thing?"

"*Oui,*" he says; the only French word I know. I kiss him again as he continues speaking in French, the unfamiliar words luring me into a peaceful state of semi-consciousness.

Yeah, I'm aware I'm going to fall hard for Aiden if I'm not careful, but I'll deal with that later.

CHAPTER EIGHT

The class Liam signed me up for is called "Ropecraft 101" and is being held at Gear Stop, a local leather gear store, in thirty minutes. He said he would pick me up in five, and that I should wear whatever seemed right. I'm wearing a black t-shirt, black shorts and my black gym shoes. It's 118 degrees outside, so I forego any attempt at jeans and boots.

Liam pulls up in his silver BMW SUV. I get in the passenger seat to find Aiden sitting behind me.

"You're joining us?"

Aiden leans forward. "I'm your rope bunny."

I glance at Liam.

"Surely, you didn't think you were going to practice on me."

"At least you would have been a challenge."

Liam runs his fingers through my hair. "You're going to be trouble someday soon."

We arrive at the store a little early, which is always my preference. I learn we are joining six other pairs of clueless ropesters, as they call themselves. The store isn't much bigger than Liam and Rik's dungeon, but much more crowded with merchandise. Liam introduces me to Master Ryker, the store owner who—no surprise—he knows well. Master Ryker is a shorter lean black man in his early forties with a shaved head. He's sexy as fuck in his black leather chaps over faded jeans and a blue leather vest over a black t-shirt. He has a high, sweet voice and keeps calling Aiden and I "darling." Like so many men in Palm Springs, he is extremely fit.

Glancing around, I notice Aiden and I are the youngest in the room by a good twenty years.

My eyes and dick notice a burly man wearing jeans, a grey t-shirt, cowboy boots and a white cowboy hat. He has a big, muscular chest and a reddish-blond beard. "Who's that?" I ask Liam.

Liam chuckles. "Damn, boy; you certainly have a type."

I can't help but grin.

"That's Cowboy," Liam whispers. "Master Ryker's husband. His real name is David Maddox, but everyone in town just calls him Cowboy."

"Yee haw."

"They met when they both lived in Tennessee, but moved here in 2008 when same-sex marriage became legal in California. They have a horse ranch in Pinyon Pines, which is thirty miles or so south/southwest of here. Cowboy runs the ranch. Master Ryker spends most of his time running this store."

Aiden elbows me. "I tried to ride that bronco, but he's apparently all bottom."

"How terrible for me," I mumble with a smile.

Liam pokes me in the ribs. "Definitely trouble."

I look around the store and am drawn to a rack of leather armbands which have multiple snaps to fit, I presume, different sized arms. I retrieve a black one and clumsily snap it around my right bicep. It feels sexy.

"Everyone line up," Liam announces to the room. "Caine wants to be abused."

"Finally," Aiden says as he hops behind me and grabs my hips. "Bend over, bitch."

I swat him away with a laugh. "Where did that come from?"

"The different colors indicate your preferred fetish or preference. Wearing them on your right side indicates you're the bottom, receiver, or submissive of said fetish, the left side identifies you as the top, giver, or dominant."

I unsnap the leather strap and stare at it. "Jesus. Who makes this shit up?"

"Old hankey code from the 70's," Liam explains. "Men would wear a colored handkerchief, or several, in either their left or right back pocket to let other men know what they were looking for."

"Clever old fucks, eh?" Aiden drawls.

"No shit," I agree. "What do the different colors mean?"

Liam points to the strap in my hand. "Interesting choice as black is for S&M, generally very heavy S&M."

"Dang, I just grabbed it because it matched my shirt."

"Hmm," is Liam's only reply as he snaps it around my left bicep.

"So black is your color as well?"

Liam nods. "Black and navy blue, as navy indicates anal sex." What about Aiden?"

"Light blue, to match my eyes."

Liam reaches up for a light blue strap and secures it around Aiden's right arm. "Light blue indicates oral sex, which is appropriate. Aiden will blow every person in this room if we let him."

"It's too tight," Aiden complains as he flexes his bicep. "Is there a color for show-off?"

"Not that I'm aware, but there should be." Liam points to a red one. "Red is for fisting. That's Rik's favorite."

"Wow. Giving or receiving?"

"Yes."

"Damn. At least he has small hands. My hands would kill someone."

Liam smiles. "We'll see." He points back to the rack. "Grey is for bondage, so that one is appropriate for today. Yellow is for watersports."

"He doesn't mean waterskiing," Aiden says with a laugh.

I'm aware watersports refers to piss-play but I keep quiet and continue listening to Liam.

"Beige is for rimming."

"Yes, please."

Liam smiles at me. "Kelly green indicates prostitution, either as a hustler or someone looking to rent one depending on the arm." Liam glances at Aiden, who shrugs without comment. "Brown is for Scat."

"No, thank you."

Liam laughs. "That's not my cup of tea, either. Remember not to judge others in the fetish community, though; there's something for everyone."

Master Ryker announces the class is about to begin and instructs us to pair off in a semi-circle. "Welcome to Ropecraft 101. Let's go over basic rules of conduct before getting too tied up in the subject."

Several people laugh politely.

"The first subject to address is always informed consent. Bondage without consent is akin to rape so I will say it again: informed consent. This is more than someone nodding when you ask if you can restrain them; it means you have a conversation about your mutual goals and expectations and make sure all parties involved understand what the scene will entail. This is integral so you and your partner can negotiate what is acceptable and what is a hard no. This brings us to the subject of safe words: everyone should establish a safe word before a bondage scene."

Aiden nudges me. "My safe word is jambalaya. Shit, now I'm hungry."

"You're insane," I whisper.

"If gags are to be incorporated into a session," Master Ryker continues while glaring at us, "a safe signal is required so that there is a non-verbal way to communicate when the scene must stop."

Master Ryker holds up a pair of scissors similar to yet bigger than the bandage scissors I always carry with me at work. "Next is safety scissors. Everyone needs a way to cut away the rope if something goes wrong. One time in San Fransico, one of my subs had a seizure during our session and became unconscious. I imagined what the scene would look to emergency services and was torn between what to do first: cut my sub free or call 911." He points to me. "Everything turned out fine but we aren't all nurses like Caine here, so be sure you are prepared for any scenario."

Everyone's eyes are on me for a few seconds. I feel naked.

Master Ryker turns to a table behind him and lifts a cord

of rope. "Let's talk about rope basics. The thinner the rope, the more it will hurt. Thicker rope is more comfortable, but it makes bulky knots. My favorite is eight-millimeter diameter, which is what we will use today. As for length, there's no right or wrong. I recommend you have several lengths to work with. Ten feet long works great for wrists and ankles, or tying limbs to a bedpost. Fifteen feet works well around thighs—maybe not Aiden's thighs, but for normal people."

Aiden flexes and bows to the participants.

"A thirty-foot length a rope is best for harnesses and suspension work. Different types of rope have different tooth. The term tooth refers to the grab of a rope. The more tooth it has, the less likely it will slip. Lower tooth ropes tend to be less prickly and are more comfortable, so it all depends on what you and your partner enjoy."

Master Ryker holds up three different cords of rope. "There is a variety of rope composition and, like most things, the one you use is a matter of preference. Cotton rope is usually the cheapest. It's reasonably light and has pretty good tooth, so the knots can be difficult to untie. Many people prefer cotton because it is so cheap they can simply cut it off and throw it away after each session. Nylon rope is more expensive than cotton. It tends to be smooth and comes in many colors. Nylon rope is what we will use today. Hemp rope is often the favorite in the scene: it has great tooth, is all natural, but can be very expensive."

I nod slowly.

Master Ryker motions to a display table behind us. "Everyone take a cord of rope. These are fifteen-foot lengths and, as I mentioned, nylon."

Aiden hands me our rope with a goofy smile.

"Let's start by taking our rope and folding it in the middle so that both ends match up," Master Ryker instructs. "The folded section is referred to as the bight, and the other side where the two ends come together is called the working end."

Ryker walks up to Aiden and pulls him toward the table. "Let's use this muscle-boy a bit. Aiden, would you be so kind as to remove your shirt?"

Aiden unsnaps his grey flannel shirt, folds it neatly, and sets it on the table. Several men whistle and cat call and I'm surprised to feel, what ..., jealousy?"

Liam, who is standing against a wall to our left, gives me side-eye. Again, I am convinced this man can read my mind.

"I'm going to teach all of you a single column tie. A column refers to your body parts; your arms and legs are columns, as is your torso. Your neck is a column, but only true masters should use rope on the neck for obvious reasons. Ropecraft, often referred to as the Japanese art of shibari, is all about connecting these columns with rope. It can get very detailed, but we will keep it simple today."

We are taught how to tie a Burlington bowline. The knot looks easy enough when Master Ryker ties it around Aiden's thigh, but took most of us several attempts to master. Liam assisted us with it and I'm proud to say I am better at it than Aiden. We spend the next hour learning a few tricks by using this one particular knot in various ways.

"This is more complicated than I imagined," I whisper to Liam.

Liam pats my arm, suddenly reminding me of my wrestling coach. Damn, Coach Gonzales was a sexy man. "It takes practice. That's why we have a dungeon."

As much as I love the idea of bondage, the closest I've come to a bondage scene was when Glenn allowed me to use his handcuffs on him in a bar in Sante Fe. I am nervous in front of all these strangers and clearly have no idea what I'm doing, but it actually turns out to be fun. After class, Liam picks out a few cords of rope, safety scissors, and a black neoprene blindfold as well as the black leather strap I still have around my left arm.

Master Ryker approaches us at the register. "Liam's money is no good here," he says to the moody-looking guy at the register. "Are you boys hitting beer bust?"

Liam turns to me. "Want to go to the raunchiest leather-bar in town for some cheap beer?"

"He does," Aiden answers. "Maybe we can practice our bondage skills on a hot daddy."

I laugh. "Lead the way, Sir."

◆ ◆ ◆

I ask Liam to stop at a drive thru ATM for tip money before we drive south several miles to Cathedral City. The Barracks bar is the desert's largest leather bar and has a beer bust every Sunday, where five dollars provides unlimited beer between two and eight. Liam escorts us through the door, past the main bar which is all corrugated steel with a biker-bar vibe, and outside to the patio bar. The line for this bar is several men deep, much shorter than the main bar inside. The music is a mix of disco and 90's dance. I expected heavy metal based on the look and smell of this place. There's a good mix of people of various age crowding the patio. Liam notices me gawking and offers to be my guide.

"The younger men in shorts and polo shirts are visiting from Los Angeles. You can always spot the LA boys because they insist on wearing collared shirts on weekends regardless of the heat. The ones there with the pastel shorts are probably from San Diego, maybe Orange County. Most of the older men in leather are locals and most of the younger leather boys are here looking for daddies."

A man who has to be in his eighties walks by wearing nothing but a black leather jockstrap.

"Scared?" Aiden asks with a nudge.

"I'm a nurse. I've seen worse. Besides," I wave back to the man who notices me watching him, "fucking good for him, right?"

"Exactly," Liam says with a pat on my shoulder. "Everyone should be included in the fun."

"Will Rik be joining us?"

"Not tonight?"

"Because he doesn't drink?"

Liam shakes his head and yells over the music. "As you may

have guessed, he is a recovering alcoholic and hasn't had a drink in seven years. That being said, he loves coming here and claims to have no issue being around drinkers. It wasn't always like that. Anyway, he's not joining us because it is a summer weekend and there are too many tourists who would recognize him." Liam nods his head towards Aiden, who is flexing for a random man. "Unlike our boy here, Rik doesn't enjoy the attention of strangers."

I nod and can actually imagine how annoying it must be for someone like Rik in a public place. While I doubt anyone outside of the gay community would recognize him, he would be a super-star in this bar.

Aiden rejoins us and pushes me forward towards the bar. We order beer drawn from a keg and served in plastic cups. Stepping aside to a small table, I allow myself to soak in the good energy. This place is fun, with little pretense, and everyone seems relaxed. Still, I'm nervous around all of these men. I down my beer, feeling out of place.

We go back to the bar for another round. Aiden takes his shirt off and tucks it into the back of his shorts. The men Liam pointed out as visitors are drawn to Aiden and we are quickly in a circle of ten or so men who go out of their way to explain how important they are and how much money they make. I find the exchange very unsexy and focus on Aiden. He seems to love the attention but a quick flash of eye contact tells me he's just playing a role. It's easy to forget he is shy because he's so good at pretending otherwise. I back away towards Liam and watch the circle of men try to impress Aiden.

"Overwhelmed?" Liam asks as he hands me a fresh beer.

"Just the right amount of whelm." I love the variety of men in this place but notice the men who are most-likely locals keep their distance from Aiden. "Are they avoiding Aiden because he is your boy?"

"Very observant, yes, though he is allowed to play with anyone he wants. He is our son, not our slave."

"I see."

"He's a hard read, even for me. Aiden's probably showing

off to those men to impress you without a clue it's making you jealous."

I down the cold beer without comment.

Liam rubs my shoulders. "You, sweet boy, are not as difficult to read."

"Oh?"

"You let yourself fall for him."

"Oh."

"Against my advice."

"Maybe, yes."

"Aiden is a beautiful boy but will never be what you want him to be. Enjoy him while you are here and then use what you learned in the next city you land in. Have you decided on your next contract?"

"No, and I need to decide soon. I'm torn between Denver and Seattle: Both have nice weather in the summer and pay the same. I've never been to either city."

"What does your gut tell you?"

"Hmm. Denver is a little closer of a drive, four hours less. Colorado is a compact state, which means my New Mexico nursing license is valid there. Also, I could visit my parents on the way to Denver."

"I don't want to sway you either way. That being said, I can put you in a suite at our hotel if you end up choosing Denver."

I pull my eyes away from Aiden and face Liam. "I could never ask for such—"

"You didn't ask, and Rik and I would insist. I told you, Caine: you are part of this family."

"Thank you, Sir."

"Now stop fucking your little brother."

"Oh my god."

Liam laughs. "I'm joking. Fuck him every day if it makes you happy. Now let's get you another beer."

This patio bar has become packed so Liam guides me further back to a smaller, temporary bar which only serves beer. There's a woman wearing a spandex catsuit and a white sailor's cap barbequing hot dogs on a grill beside the bar.

"Now I've seen everything."

"Oh, it's just getting started. This place will be a madhouse on July fourth."

"The dinner you have planned for us sounds nice enough."

"Oh, perfect timing," Liam says as Master Ryker and Cowboy join us. "Caine was just asking about the fourth."

Ryker looks up at me. "It's a charity event I've hosted the past few years. You'll love it."

A shirtless guy with dark hair and light grey eyes pushes past Cowboy to stand next to me at the bar. He's wearing yellow boots, black lycra shorts and has a chain and pad lock around his neck. He checks me out from head to toe and smiles. "Yummy."

His eyes glow in a way that makes me think he is high. He has great teeth, though, and big pink nipples that remind me of Aiden. "Uh, hi," I say.

Hey reaches under my shirt and begins pulling it over my head. "It's too hot for this shirt."

I glance at Liam for help but all he does is raise his eyebrows and smile. Fighting the urge to resist, I set my beer on the bar and allow this guy to remove my shirt.

"That's more like it."

I'm curious about the padlock and reach for it. Liam lightly grabs my wrist and pulls my hand away. The guy looks at me, then Liam, then shrugs and kisses me on the mouth, quick and without passion. "Have a fun night, sexy." He hands me my shirt and sinks into the crowd.

I turn to Liam. "What the hell was that?"

Liam shakes his head. "I've never seen him before but he is a sexy fucker. It's disrespectful, by the way, to touch any form of lock they may be wearing."

"Why?"

Master Ryker leans in. "Some people just wear them for show, but in the fetish community it means someone owns them. You should always ask permission before touching such a lock, or even a chain necklace, until you know what it signifies."

"Yikes, I had no idea. I just thought it was sexy."

"That's why I'm here, baby-boy."

I nod and order another round of beer for all of us. It tastes like American light beer and is probably low octane, but I'm getting a little drunk so I slow my pace. That's when I notice Dr. Laughlin in the crowd. I duck behind Liam before I can stop myself.

"Who are we hiding from?"

"Ugh. One of the doctors at the hospital."

"You're worried they will see you at a gay bar?" Cowboy asks with general concern.

"No, it's not that. He's just so mean to me, so demeaning. I hate working with him."

Liam turns. "Which one?"

I point with my beer. "The tall guy with the backwards ballcap and the nice arms."

"Jason Laughlin?"

I sigh. "Of course, you know him."

Master Ryker laughs as Liam takes the beers from my hand and sets them on the bar. "Come with me."

"I don't want to cause trouble."

Liam's bright green eyes flash a wicked gleam. "Trust me, this will be fun."

"We'll guard your beer," Cowboy says in his sexy Tennessee accent.

Liam takes my hand and guides me across the patio to Dr. Laughlin, who is laughing with two men. It's interesting to see him out of the hospital because I've never thought of him as anything other than a jerk of a doctor. I had no idea he was gay, if he even is gay, but I've never given him much thought and try to avoid him at work the best I can. He's wearing a blue printed t-shirt which shows off his arms and tight chest. He's tall, maybe six-six, and his t-shirt is riding up to show off blond fuzz on his flat belly. He looks silly with his backwards baseball cap and I wonder if it's an attempt to look younger because it only makes him look older. Dr. Laughlin isn't a bad-looking guy and I always assumed he was in good shape under his lab coat due to the prominent veins in his long neck. He's blond, which really isn't my thing, with greyish-blue eyes and a long thin nose. Funny, I suspected he didn't like me because he picked up on my being gay, but here he is at a gay bar.

Dr. Laughlin stops laughing as soon as he sees Liam.

"Come with me," Liam says to Dr. Laughlin without greeting and guides me inside to an area of the bar I haven't seen and into a large bathroom.

I have no idea if Dr. Laughlin is following us and I'm afraid to turn around to check. Liam walks to the back of the bathroom and opens the wheelchair-accessible stall, indicating I enter. Dr. Laughlin enters behind me without a word as Liam joins us and closes the door. We make eye contact for the first time: he definitely recognizes me.

"On your knees, boy," Liam snarls. I begin to obey, confused, but Liam taps my chest and indicates he isn't talking to me.

"Yes, Sir," Dr. Laughlin whispers in a shaking voice. He lowers himself to his knees.

I look to Liam for guidance but he is staring down at Dr. Laughlin who, even on his knees, isn't much shorter than Liam. I have no idea what is happening. I try my best not to show my discomfort and fight my adrenaline-rushed desire to escape this crowded stall.

"I'm told you have been an asshole at work, making Caine uncomfortable."

Dr. Laughlin nods.

"Why?"

"Because of my need to feel superior," Dr. Laughlin says. "Because he makes me feel inadequate."

I'm stunned, suspecting this is a rehearsed response and that they know each other very well.

"And how does Caine make you feel inadequate?"

"He's young and sexy and people like him." Dr. Laughlin rubs his crotch and glances at me.

Holy shit: This is turning him on.

I gasp when Liam strikes Dr. Laughlin across the face. "You need to remember your place, boy."

I'm not sure if it was the slap or the way he took it without reaction, but my cock begins to pulse.

Dr. Laughlin bows his head. "Yes, Sir."

Liam turns to me and smiles. "Caine, I want you to show off your beautiful cock."

I'm horrified and certain Liam senses it, but he only nods. I maintain eye contact with Liam and try my best to pretend Dr. Laughlin isn't here. My dick is getting harder the more I try to stop it and I don't know what else to do but submit to this madness and let the scene play out as it will. I unbutton my shorts, draw the zipper down, and pull my dick out of my underwear. I'm almost fully erect at this point and sigh in embarrassment.

Dr. Laughlin stares at my dick. "I am unworthy, Sir."

The hum of bathroom noise dims and I can't help thinking everyone is listening to this exchange. I'm ashamed this is turning me on and there's no way to hide it. My stomach churns with anxiety and I feel like I just exposed my shame in front of a hundred people.

Dr. Laughlin places his hands on the dirty bathroom floor and lowers his mouth toward my dick. "Shall I suck it, Sir?

I have no idea if he's talking to me or Liam, but I can't bring myself to speak.

Liam chuckles. "And give you what you want? That doesn't sound like much of a punishment."

Liam looks up at me and rubs my chest. In that quick exchange I sense he knows I'm nervous as fuck and is encouraging me to trust him. "Caine. This unworthy pig would love to suck your huge cock, but that would be a reward he has yet to earn. Jack off for me. Use this unworthy face as a cum rag."

I inhale and restrain a shutter as Dr. Laughlin opens his mouth and sticks out his tongue. There's nothing left to do and after spending the day roping Aiden into various sexy positions, I suspect I can cum in thirty seconds.

I spit in my palm and close my eyes. I begin stroking my

cock, slowly. I've never jacked off in front of two people before and worry about performance anxiety: Will Liam be upset if I am unable to cum?

I spit on my hand again and crank faster. Liam rubs my chest, which helps. I work up the nerve to open my eyes and look down at Dr. Laughlin, who is staring up at me with his mouth wide open. He's removed his hat and his sweaty blond hair is pressed against his head. His eyes are pretty in this lighting.

My balls pull up in my gut as I get close. I grab Dr. Laughlin's face with my thumb in his mouth and do my best to aim my load. Standing on my tip toes and trying not to make noise, I shoot a hard load which splashes across his face and all over his neck. I shoot again, marking his t-shirt. Again, holding my breath until a soft groan escapes my throat. One more glob misses the mark and hits the floor near my shoes.

Panting, I rub my cock across Dr. Laughlin's stubbled chin. Liam is all smile as I push my cock back into my underwear and pull up my shorts. Liam opens the stall door to a small crowd who whoop and cheer playfully as I follow him out, leaving Dr. Laughlin on his knees in the stall. I quickly wash my hands, ignoring the guys watching me, and follow Liam. "Holy shit," I hiss once we are out of the bathroom. "What just happened?"

Liam pats me on the back and guides me back to our table. "I was trying to avoid introducing you because I knew you worked in the same hospital, but things always have a way of working themselves out. You've just been introduced to our slave."

CHAPTER NINE

ICU was slow today and I was excited when they sent me home at noon after my only patient was discharged. Not only does my contract pay me my full twelve hours whether I work or not, but today is the fourth of July and now I don't have to rush to join the guys tonight. I call Liam from my car to share the news.

"Come spend the day relaxing with us at the pool and then we can all go to dinner together."

"Perfect. I'll be there in an hour. Can I bring anything?"

Liam chuckles. "We have everything we need here except you."

Mitch and Stefani are already gone when I get home, as they are spending the night in Lake Arrowhead. I check on the dogs, take a shower, and shove what I need in my backpack before making the drive to the mansion (Liam scolds me whenever I call it that, but, give me a break). Traffic sucks on Palm Canyon so I go the back route Aiden taught me. I arrive by 1:30 to find the three of them relaxing, naked, in their giant lake of a pool.

It's 107 degrees today so there is little else to do other than strip down and join them with a splash.

"Caine's here," Aiden announces as he rolls off one of the green rafts and pulls himself out of the water. "Now we can eat."

I watch Aiden's muscled ass as he lights the barbeque and walks into the house.

"He's our chef today," Liam mumbles. He seems drowsy or drunk, though I've never seen him drunk before. I've seen Liam naked several times but this is the first time I've noticed how big his dick is. I swim up to his raft, suddenly horny, but I refrain from touching it.

"I've worked these past three days. What have I missed?"

Rik maneuvers his raft to join us. "Liam's sleepy because he abused your doctor until four this morning."

"Hmm," is all Liam gives me.

"He was extra rough because of the way he has been treating you at work."

I was wondering why Dr. Laughlin wasn't at work today. "Thanks?"

"Don't feel bad," Rik adds with a nudge to my arm. "Our slave loved it."

Liam smiles at me. I notice the ice in his drink has melted. "May I get you another drink?"

He glances down at the glass in his hand like he forgot it was there. "Indeed. Whiskey and Coke." He hands me his clear acrylic cup. "The Woodford Reserve."

I salute him and pull myself out of the pool. Aiden brushes up behind me as I make the drink. I decide to make one for myself as well.

"Happy fourth, Caine." He's wearing a black apron with the words "Call me Daddy" and is holding a tray of raw steaks.

"I'm not calling you daddy, you young punk."

Aiden rolls his eyes. "Calm down, boy. You're only four years older than me."

I can tell he's a little drunk. "Yea, but still. What's for lunch, chef?"

"T-bone, potato salad and collard greens. They asked for a light lunch so it doesn't spoil their dinner."

"Only you would consider this a light lunch. Want another drink, or have you hit your limit?

Aiden smiles shyly, a total act, and glances down at what I'm pouring. "I'll take a light one, but use Diet Coke."

"You know one of the only things worse for you than sugar is saccharine."

"Don't nurse me. I mean, you can nurse on my cock anytime, but you know what I mean."

I shake my head and watch him walk to the barbeque. He

flexes his ass, teasing me. I take a long pull from my drink and top it off, then place the three drinks and a bottle of water on a tray and carry them back to the pool. If Aiden wants it, he has to work for it.

Liam and Rik guide their rafts to the offered drinks.

"Thank you, kind sir," Rik says as he takes the water.

I hand Liam his drink. "I wouldn't have pegged you for a whiskey and coke kind of guy."

"You can take the boy out of Texas," Rik chimes.

I look to Liam for confirmation because he doesn't have a hint of a Texan accent. Come to think of it, he may have mentioned Texas. I need to work on improving my listening skills.

Liam nods. "Born and raised in San Antonio."

"Yee haw," Aiden yells from the barbeque.

"What was your childhood like?"

Liam glares at me over his sun glasses. "We lived well, but nothing like this. My childhood was the same as most gay boys': awkward, uncertain, scary. I suppose I would have been a momma's boy, but Daddy had other plans for me." Liam takes a sip. "He was stern but kind, a very dry and quiet man in a world of loud Texan men. He sold fax machines back when people had to buy two at a time so that they could both send and receive. Sounds crazy today, but there was serious money in fax machines back then."

"Is he a good man?"

Liam turns his head to the side and looks at Rik. "He was a good man, in his own way. I couldn't bring myself to come out to him until I had already moved out. I'm sure he meant well."

He tells me about his high school experience, his ex-wife, and his little brother I didn't know existed.

I nearly groan when Aiden announces lunch is ready. This is the most I've ever heard Liam share about himself and I want it to continue. We eat lunch at one of three tables under the main patio cover, out of the sun. Liam was right; Aiden is a good cook and I love whatever he did to season the steaks. After lunch, the vote is unanimous: we all need to get out of this heat and take a nap before tonight's event. Aiden leads me upstairs to his bedroom, which is like a little apartment with its own living room and bathroom. It's odd to think I've never seen his room before, or any of the bedrooms in here.

"How many bedrooms are in this place?"

"Twenty-seven." Aiden laughs at my shock. "I'm kidding. The house is a little more than 9000 square feet, but there's really only six bedrooms: four big guest suites like this one here, a regular bedroom I don't think they've ever used, and their bedroom. Their room is bigger than most houses. I guess you could also count the library as a bedroom, and the dungeon.

Aiden's room is painted a light gray-blue with black crown molding stretching up to the high white ceiling. It looks like a hotel room, and I see nothing of Aiden aside from his Xbox. "How long have you lived here?"

Aiden steps into the shower and beckons me to follow him. "Three years or so."

I join him in the shower, which is way hotter than I prefer. "Where's all your stuff?"

Aiden shrugs and points to his back. I learned during our Ropecraft 101 class that Aiden is too muscular to reach the center of his back, so I lather him up and scrub his back with the loofa he hands me. He turns around and pretends not to notice my erection as he lathers my chest. He looks into my eyes and smiles. "Uh oh, I know that look."

I feel myself blushing. "I can't help it."

As usual, all he gives me is a shrug as he slowly wraps his soapy hand around my cock. I reach down and return the favor. Aiden has a nice cock. It looks small in comparison to his massive thighs, but it's nearly as long as mine and probably just as thick.

"You're gonna make me cum," he drawls.

"Everything makes you cum. You're on a cycle of testosterone and god-knows what else."

"Hmm."

"I want to fuck you."

"Ha! You always want to fuck me."

"Hmm."

Aiden releases his grip and rinses me off in the near-scalding water. "I didn't clean my ass today," he says as he lowers himself to his knees and looks up at me. "My mouth is nice and clean, though." He splashes the soap from my dick and begins blowing me so hard my knees quiver.

I grab his head for support. "Holy shit, this isn't a race." I try taking control but his hands are a vice on my ass and he ignores my gasps and yelps as he works for my nut. Electricity courses up my spine and I become one with my cock. "Aiden! I can't hold back. You're going to make me... fuuuuuuuck." I may have screamed as Aiden drew in the first of my load. I'm sure I would have fallen if he wasn't holding me like this. "Oh my god," I gasp, pumping deep down his throat. "Oh my god. Jesus Christ. Oh, god.

Aiden finally pulls his mouth away from my cock long enough to laugh. "You get pretty religious when you cum."

I notice for the first time he is jacking off. Had he been this whole time?

"Put your dick back in my mouth."

I oblige and let him wrap his mouth around my aching dick. I can't see his dick from this angle but his body begins rocking harder and harder until the veins on his neck pop out and he moans like a possessed bear.

◆ ◆ ◆

I wake to Aiden's phone alarm, staring at the light freckles on his muscular back. We napped for an hour but it feels like we've been sleeping all day. We rinse off in the shower, make ourselves presentable, and make our way down the stairs to find Liam and Rik sitting in the living room. I'm pretty sure this is the first time I've seen anyone in this room.

Liam's plan for us tonight is dinner and fireworks at The O'Donnell House, which I'm told is a historic home from the 1920's which is now used as an event venue for weddings and corporate parties. Mitch and Stephani said they have been to a wedding there and that the view is amazing. Tonight's event is the fundraiser Master Ryker told us about and we will be sitting at his table. We will be dining outside in this crazy heat, which is why Rik purchased sweat-wicking polo shirts for us. All I can do is shake my head as Rik hands us our shirts. Liam's is black, Rik's is red, Aiden's is powder blue, and mine is gray. "What a coincidence," I laugh.

"There are no coincidences, young man. You will learn that for yourself one day."

Rik drives us to the event in a red Jeep Grand Cherokee I have never seen before. "How many cars do you guys have?"

"Just this and Liam's BMW. I also have a motorcycle."

I don't know why, but I can't picture Rik on a motorcycle. "Which type."

"It's a silver Indian Scout," Aiden says. "Rik lets me ride it. I bet you want to wrap your arms around my muscles as we ride off into the sunset."

"Do they make helmets big enough for your head?"

Aiden laughs. "Seriously, though. Let me take you to Joshua Tree before you leave. You will love it."

Rik parks a few minutes before sunset. The O'Donnell House is a large mediterranean house perched high on the mountain face. I count six long tables which each have seating for twenty lined up at an interesting angle along the edge of the large deck, presumably to provide everyone a view of the fireworks. I was nervous this event would be fancy, but am relieved to see people dressed in casual attire such as shorts and Hawaiian shirts.

"I should have worn sandals," Aiden whispers in my ear.

Liam introduces me to several people I'll never remember. I do my best to look interested in what is being said until Master Ryker joins us and escorts us to the centermost table. Cowboy is already seated and is talking with a beautiful older woman I'm pretty sure is a movie star.

"Is that?" I whisper to Aiden.

"Yup. She was huge in the seventies, then got crazy-rich selling exercise equipment. You're probably old enough to remember her show."

I reach between us and punch his dick. "I'm four years older than you."

He kisses the back of my neck. "Whatever, daddy."

Name cards in the shape of stars indicate where each of us should sit, with Aiden and I sitting directly across from Liam and Rik. Young men in tuxedos who must be miserable in this heat pass around water and wine. It feels like a wedding reception.

Master Ryker stands and draws the attention of the crowd. He gives a short speech about the generosity of the attendees and how the funds raised today will assist troubled youth through the Greater Palm Spring's LGBTQ community center, known as The Center. He raises his glass of water over his head and wishes everyone a wonderful evening. I watch him move around each of the tables, encouraging everyone to eat. He's very good with people. After making his rounds, he stands behind me and rubs my shoulders as he talks to Liam and Rik. "You boys look so handsome tonight," he says in his high voice. "Thank you for joining us."

Rik winks at me, making me blush.

Master Ryker and Cowboy sit next to Liam and begins discussing the hotel Liam and Rik are opening in Key West next year. It is clear Liam and Rik know the movie star. I shouldn't be surprised, as they seem to know everyone in this town. Aiden elbows me and I follow him to the buffet table.

"I don't know about you," Aiden drawls as he piles food onto his plate, "but I feel uncomfortable listening to them talk about their business. I feel like I'm spying on them, you know?"

I do know, and feel the same way. It's like their business personas are people I don't even know. Liam once explained his work as just that: work, and nothing more. A means to an end. He suggested I never take my job too seriously and to spend at least as much time working on myself and my passions as I do on any job.

Aiden is politely chatting with someone as his pile of food gets higher.

"I'm sure they will give you a second plate."

Aiden laughs like I'm ridiculous. "This plate is plenty big. You'll see."

Rik covers his eyes with his hand when he sees Aiden's skyscraper of a meal. "You'd think we were starving the boy"

Liam laughs. I think he enjoys watching Aiden eat. I certainly do. I can't pull my eyes away as he meticulously cracks open each of the crab legs without making a mess and arranges the meat on his plate like a chef.

I'm drinking too much wine because of this heat and am a little drunky by the time the fireworks begin. Aiden picks up on it and caresses my ass as the crowd "ooohs" and "ahhhhs" as though they've never seen fireworks before. He's turning me on, which seems super inappropriate here, but I don't stop him.

I look out at the vista in front of me, the sprawl of Coachella Valley illuminated by the firework display. I only have two more shifts left in this contract and have to make a decision about my next one. I turn to Aiden, who is still rubbing my ass and looking up at the fireworks with the wonderment of a child. I fear leaving this desert life almost as much as I fear getting too attached to it. I'm nowhere near ready to settle down and have so much more to learn.

Still, the thought of leaving in a few weeks is heavy.

Aiden turns to me with a big smile and kisses my cheek. I wish Aiden could come with me.

I wish Aiden wanted to come with me.

CHAPTER TEN

R andy and I have been alternating chest compressions for the past thirty minutes without achieving a pulse. I doubt there's any hope for my patient at this point but we continue doing everything we can. I'm guessing Dr. Laughlin would have called it long ago if not for the patient's wife and daughter standing outside the room, screaming for us to save him. The wife keeps yelling at us to shock him but I can't break focus long enough to explain we don't defibrillate patients in asystole. The House Supervisor is there with them but he seems pretty useless. Tonight's code team is great but even the best of codes are chaotic messes of people yelling over each other and shifting positions in this small ICU room.

"Pulse check," the charge nurse calls out and I stop compressions with a gasp. I press my gloved fingers against the patient's neck while another nurse uses a doppler to scan for a femoral pulse. I glance at Dr. Laughlin who is running the code from the foot of the bed and shake my head. "No pulse, doctor. Resume compressions?"

He nods.

"Resuming compressions," I call out to the room as I continue chest compressions.

"Resuming compressions at 18:37," Randy shouts out for benefit of the recorder.

I try not to grimace as I feel the sternum pop under my hands. Breaking ribs is not uncommon during chest compressions but it still freaks me out every time. The respiratory therapist at the head of the bed looks up at me, making me wonder if she heard the bones break.

The charge nurse announces three minutes have passed since the fifth dose of epinephrine. "Let's give one more epi," Dr. Laughlin announces. He sounds resigned and looks as tired as I feel. We usually stop after the fifth injection of epinephrine, but another dose isn't going to hurt. It's not going to help, either.

Randy taps me on the back and we switch places on the count of ten. I step behind Randy and out of everyone's way as I catch my breath. As odd as it has been working with Dr. Laughlin after that bathroom scene two weeks ago, I've learned I can depend on him during crisis. He may be an asshole, but he is a competent doctor. I can't look at him without being flooded with the image of him looking up at me in appreciation as I dumped my load all over his face, but he's been great at not treating me differently. Well ... he no longer yells at me, but he remains professional.

Another pulse check is called and I switch places with Randy.

"Nothing," I say as quiet as I can get away with. I can't help watch my patient's family falling apart outside the room. Dr. Laughlin catches my eye and nods. "Let's go, people."

"Resuming compressions," I say.

"Resuming compressions at 1841," I hear in a blur as though I am underwater. I focus on my heartbeat as the robotic voice of the cardiac monitor drones *good compressions, good compression, good compressions.*

Randy pulls on my shoulder and it takes me a moment to realize its already time for another pulse check. There's no pulse, the skin is cold and has started to mottle a strange blotchy purple I have only seen with death. I look at Dr. Laughlin.

"I feel we have done everything available to us for Mr. Williams," Dr. Laughlin says, "and recommend we cease all lifesaving efforts." Dr. Laughlin looks drained of energy. "Does anyone in this room disagree with this recommendation?"

I shake my head and turn to the patient's family as they are escorted bedside. Dr. Laughlin explains the situation as I continue compressions until the wife nods. I stop compressions and the wife screams something horrible and unintelligible as Dr. Laughlin calls time of death. I step further back as the wife and daughter throw themselves on the patient. I give a nod to Randy and the rest of the team in what I hope conveys "good job and thank you."

Trying to be invisible, I remove all the empty syringes from the patient's bed and lift the sheets up to his neck in an attempt to make him look less horrifying. This will be his family's last image of him. I do what little I can to make it better.

Dr. Laughlin pats my shoulder as I pass by him to leave the room. I glance up to him and, in that flash of a moment, see a completely different person. It figures we would finally connect on my last day working here.

◆ ◆ ◆

I park my car in front of the house and drop my head on the steering wheel. It's nearly ten at night and I am numb. I drag myself though the side gate into the backyard to find Mitch in green speedos, drinking from a bottle of whiskey. He asks me to join him but all I need right now is a long hot shower. After what feels like an hour I step out of the shower, pull on my board shorts, and return to the pool.

"Bad day?" Mitch asks as I lower myself into the pool.

He's drunk, so I simply nod.

"This was your last shift, right?"

I sigh. "It was an eventful last day."

"Need a drink? Stephani's out of town, so I can drink myself into a stupor."

I nod again and join him. He attempts to stand and hand me a glass but I stop him. He's very drunk and suddenly looks like a little boy. I take a hard pour of the Kentucky whiskey and drop into the lounge chair next to him. I tell him I lost a patient but avoid any details: people outside of healthcare rarely understand what an ICU shift can look like and I've learned it's best to let them think the worst complaint I have is that my feet are sore. They are sore, but I'm used to it. I feel empty, but I'm used to that as well.

I look up at the stars, clear and bright but never as much as in New Mexico. There's just too much light here, too much noise.

Mitch mumbles something and drops his glass, which bounces across the concrete. Now I know why Stephani insists on plastic glassware out here. I watch his chiseled furry chest rise and fall with each breath for fifteen minutes before diagnosing him: shit-faced and passed out. I don't know what he went through this week and I never will, but he looks more human at this moment, more relatable, than he ever has to me before. My eyes trace down his lean torso until they reach his bulge.

I look away, embarrassed. He's still sleeping and doesn't notice.

I glance at his speedos again and recall Liam asking me what I'm ashamed of.

There's no shame in being attracted to Mitch. I'm sure most people—male and female—are attracted to him and I doubt many could resist glancing at his ridiculously large bulge.

Seriously, what is going on down there?

I know what my shame is even while I try denying it. I'm ashamed of being gay because my father made me feel it was dirty; my attraction to men a perversion. My father's a good man, but I don't think he will ever let go of his anger toward me for never giving him grandchildren. I remember explaining once that I could still have children. That conversation did not go well.

I let go of a breath I didn't realize I had been holding all this time. My eyes lock on Mitch's closed eyes and my breathing synchronizes with his gentle snoring. Time stops as I reach out and run the back of my fingers against his arm.

No reaction.

I sit up and turn so that my feet are on the ground and I am on the side of the lounge, facing Mitch. The lightest thought of sliding on top of him makes my cock so hard it hurts. I rub my dick through my wet bathing suit and continue staring like a complete idiot for a good five minutes while wrestling with my better judgment.

My better judgment loses the match as I stand and hover over him. I maneuver to his side and drop to my knees. My hand reaches out as though of its own will and touches his bicep. My pulse quickens but Mitch continues his light snoring without reaction. Tracing my fingers up his arm and across his neck, I stop with my hand resting on his hard chest.

I lean forward without a breath and brush my lips across his hairy forearm. I can't stop myself from pulling my throbbing cock out of my suit, my eyes locked on his bulge. I lick his arm, tasting salt and whiskey. My tongue moves to his bicep and traces a long vein up to his shoulder.

I hover in this position, afraid to look at his face, and begin masturbating.

All I can think is that I am completely insane. I lean forward, imagining Mitch's cock in my mouth, imagining Stephani walking in to find me pinned under him as he is pumping a load down my throat. I flick my tongue over Mitch's nipple and I swear his cock begins to swell under his tight green speedos.

My aching balls pull up tight as I get close to shooting. I lick him again, a little harder this time, making his cock bounce. I slowly turn my head against his chest, daring to look at his face. My left hand squeezes my dick as my right hovers over his stomach so close I can feel his belly hair.

I move to touch his crotch when Mitch wakes with a gasp and grabs the back of my head, holding me against his chest as his eyes slowly focus on me. I can't bring myself to take a breath.

It takes him a few seconds to focus on me. His body tenses as he seems to realize what is happening.

Fuck! I can't believe I put myself in this situation.

"Caine?" Mitch mumbles, sounding somewhat like an accusation rather than a question. "What the fuck are you doing?"

I don't make a sound: there's nothing I can possibly say to make this right.

Mitch's muscular body is tense but he looks more confused than angry. Hopefully, he is too drunk to make sense of this ridiculous situation. I quickly weigh my options and choose the path of greatest resistance and greatest potential reward. Mitch isn't a violent man and I figure the worst that he'll do is knock me away.

That, and kick me out of his house.

I hesitate for a second before slowly lifting my left leg onto his lounge chair. Mitch doesn't punch me, so I drag my other leg up. Adrenaline pounds my ears as I pull my head out from under his arm and sit up so that I am straddling his waist. I look down at Mitch's beautiful eyes and can't tell if he is wondering what the hell I am doing or if he is too drunk to know what is happening.

His eyes follow my hands as I rest them on his chest. A realization strikes me like a profound truth: I have to kiss him. I lower my head, bracing for the punch. I just can't stop myself. I'm moving in slow motion, like one of those dreams where your whole body feels like it's moving through molasses, and I swear it takes me five minutes to bring my mouth to his.

My lips brush across his. It's not so much a kiss as a connection, and I'm not aware of any part of my body except the portion of my lips which are touching him. I don't move—I don't think I can—and I don't take a breath until Mitch grasps my neck and softly pushes us apart.

He looks up at me, confusion clouding his sharp eyes. The sensation of his hands on my neck travels directly to my cock. I lean in to kiss him again but he holds me back. "Please," I whisper as though I can will him to want me.

Mitch shakes his head. "You're a child."

"I'm twenty-six," I remind him. "I want this."

He smirks and relaxes his grip, lowering me towards him. "Your father's going to come after me with a shotgun."

I'm so close to his mouth I can smell the whiskey on his breath. "He doesn't own a shotgun, and he's seven hundred miles away."

Mitch hesitates a moment. I freeze, unable to read him. The corner of his mouth twitches and he shakes his head before pulling me down into a deep kiss. I wrap my legs around him and grab his hair as he twists us around so that he is in top of me. Something is jabbing into my back but I ignore it, unwilling to break away from the kiss. Instead of pulling away, Mitch pushes me down under the weight of his muscular body and pushes his tongue down my throat. I'm aware Mitch is married and how wrong this should be, yet my mind explodes with how right and perfectly natural this feels.

He rubs his big hands over the smooth skin of my chest before pinning my arms to my side. He kisses my neck, hard yet passionate. My skin ignites as his stubbled chin works down my neck, down my chest, until he is licking my stomach. This mass of a man is probably no stronger than I am, but he exudes a strength that locks me in place like a spell. I struggle to break away and want to touch him so much I may scream.

My toes find the waistband of his speedos and he laughs when I yank them down around his knees. I feel him kick them off as he finally releases my hands to pull my suit off as well. My cock is on fire, and I glance down between us to see Mitch's fat cock is as hard as mine. I lean up and kiss him again, my hands moving over the tight muscles of his arms and shoulders. He feels so different than Aiden. He smells different. I reach around his neck and pull him towards me, but he is so strong all I end up doing is pulling myself up towards him.

Mitch grinds his cock against mine. "We're crazy."

I nod, concentrating on not letting the touch of his cock make me shoot.

"I want to make you cum," Mitch growls.

"You're married."

This seems to surprise him. He kisses me again and presses my legs apart with his thighs. "You're not saying no, though."

"I'm not saying no." I reach down and stroke his cock, which is no longer than mine but twice as thick.

Mitch spits on his hand and wraps it around both of our dicks.

"Go slow," I plead. "I'm already so close."

He nods, his eyes ablaze. He rubs my cheek and kisses me

again, tender and soft. "Believe it or not," he whispers, "I have been aching to touch you since the day you moved in."

I'm removed from the reality of this moment and have to concentrate on remembering to breathe. He maneuvers himself so that he is gripping both of our cocks in one hand while holding himself up with the other.

He kisses me again. "I want to fuck you, but I can't."

I nod and actually want that as well. "I understand."

"I want you to cum with me. I want you to cum as though I am fucking a load out of you."

I nod again, lost in his eyes. I'm stupefied.

He tightens his grip on our dicks and begins stroking. He kisses me again, pushing his tongue deep in my mouth as though he could not survive without this connection. I wrap my legs around his waist and imagine what it must feel like to have his giant dick up my ass. The sensation of his dick squeezed against mine is overwhelming. I grab onto his muscular back and try not to cry out as he strokes away, bringing me closer and closer to the edge. He has a look of amazement I assume I share as he pumps his dick against mine.

I begin to cum without warning, so hard it aches deep inside my ass. I try so hard not to scream that I make a horrible screeching sound in his mouth. Mitch suddenly breaks free and arches his back as he looks up at the sky. I feel his body tremble as his mouth opens like a dog howling at the moon. Hot cum splashes all over my stomach as Mitch silently convulses through his orgasm.

Minutes pass in seconds. Mitch's muscles eventually relax and he drops his weight upon me, panting.

"Holy fuck, kid," he finally groans. I'm prepared for him to finally come to his senses and tell me how wrong this is. I'm prepared for him to deny it ever happened, or claim he was too drunk to remember any of this. I don't care, though. I am on fire and my skin vibrates with pleasure. It was worth it, regardless of the repercussions.

Rather than make excuses, Mitch looks down at me in

wonder and pulls me into another long kiss. "Yeah," he finally says, "your father is definitely going to kill us."

I smile, already wanting to make him cum again. "I suggest we don't tell him about this, then."

CHAPTER ELEVEN

Thursday evening at the mansion. My contract at the hospital ended last week and I start orientation at Denver Memorial this coming Monday. I originally planned to spend the week between contracts with my parents but, with Liam's encouragement, I stayed here. They gave me an amazing room with a view of the pool, identical to Aiden's room but painted sage green. I've spent the past four nights in Aiden's bed.

The plan today is to practice my roping skills in the dungeon. Aiden is my practice dummy, or "rope bunny" as he likes to call it. I still can't figure out if Aiden messes around with me because he likes it, or because Liam and Rik demand it. I've had so many opportunities to ask him about their situation, but I keep talking myself out of it. It's a valid concern, but I'm going to try and enjoy myself today without overthinking.

Rik has been in town all week, but Liam just returned from Key West this morning. He explained their newest property is turning out to be more difficult than the others but that they finally have achieved forward momentum, whatever that means. He and Rik have been in their room all day, so Aiden and I have been out at the pool. The plan is to meet in the dungeon at four. Aiden wanted to get ready for the dungeon session, so he went up to his room an hour ago. Preparing his ass for sex seems to be the only thing he is semi-shy about, so I'm reading a book in the library.

Liam joins me around three-thirty. "Always in a book."

"I've nearly completed this entire series while here in the desert."

Liam sits in an oversized chair across the room from me. "Have you and Aiden eaten?"

"He said he wants to do the bondage session on an empty stomach. He's grilling steaks for us tonight."

Liam groans. "I don't know if you've ever had to deal with a hungry Aiden, but I suggest we start soon before he kills one of us."

"Oh brother."

"From what I remember, he gets even more horny when he's hungry."

From what he remembers? I don't know why, but I just assumed they still mess around with Aiden. It feels like the more I learn, the less I understand.

Liam texts Rik. I know, because I've seen him do it many times. This house is so big they need to communicate through their phones. "Rik and Aiden will meet us in the dungeon. Are you ready?"

"Yup. I'm excited."

Liam looks at my hardon poking up through my basketball shorts. "I see that. Let's go."

I set my book down on the table and follow him down the spiral stairs to the dungeon. Rik is already here, setting out various cords of rope and gear. He's wearing black sweat shorts and a grey tank top which shows off his tights muscles. I can't stop thinking about that first time we met, and how hot it was to fuck him. Rik treats me like his son, but I have to keep reminding myself he's only thirty-four. I don't know where I stand with him now.

"What?" Rik asks with a smile.

"Caine feels conflicted," Liam announces. "He respects you as a mentor, yet can't help but want to fuck you."

"Jesus," I bark. "Are you psychic?"

Liam chuckles. "It's all over your face. You're very easy to read."

"Oh, sorry."

"A beautiful young man wants to fuck me," Rik says. "How terrible for me."

"It's just, confusing. And a little overwhelming."

Liam kisses the back of Rik's head. "Of course. A few months ago, you had only had sex with two men. Now you've had sex with two more, both of whom live in this house with you. Three more, if you count what you did to your doctor's face."

"Jesus."

"Four more," Rik says with a wicked smile, "if you count what he did with his landlord."

I shake my head. "You should see him. I can't even be near him without wanting to climb on top of him."

"Caine has a thing for us straight men," Aiden says from the doorway. He's wearing nothing but a black jockstrap and doesn't have any product in his hair. I've never seen him walk around with it flat like this. It makes him look even younger.

"You're about as straight as I am." I lightly punch his thick chest, leaving a white mark on his pink skin. "You got sunburned today."

He nods. "We stayed out too long."

I poke his chest. "You're the only person in Palm Springs who isn't tan."

Aiden shrugs. "I don't have your Italian genes."

"We have to paint his skin for his bodybuilding competitions," Rik says as he assesses Aiden's sunburn. "He looks weird when he's painted brown like that."

"It's more of an orange," Liam adds. "Your burn isn't that bad, but you're really going to feel the rope."

Aiden nods. "Be gentle with me."

Rik sets aside the cotton rope he originally had out and switches to black nylon. "Caine can be as rough as he wants, but this nylon rope won't tear into you as much." He looks up at Aiden, who looks a little nervous. "Have you ever been roped down before?"

Again, I'm surprised Rik would have to ask such a question. I imagined them having roped him down to this bondage bed hundreds of times.

Aiden shakes his head. "My first time was at that bondage class."

"He has serious trust issues," Liam says, running his hands through Aiden's hair. "I love when you leave your hair fluffy like this."

Aiden smirks. "That's why I cleaned it, Sir."

"Are you sure you're okay with me roping you down today?"

He nods. "I'm looking forward to seeing what you do with me when I can't overpower you. Just don't spank or whip me."

Liam pats Aiden's shoulder. "Get down on your knees."

Aiden drops down without protest. I initially think it's a sign of subservience, but then I see what Liam is doing with the rope Rik hands him. Liam folds the rope over the back of Aiden's neck and loops each end under his arms and around his back. Aiden's too tall for Liam to do this while he's standing.

"See this," Liam asks as he crosses the rope around the front of Aiden's chest. "This is a safe way to use his neck. Never loop it around the front."

I nod, stepping forward. The sight of the black rope across Aiden's smooth, pink skin is electrifying. I both hate and love the effect Aiden's body has on me.

Rik pats my erection. "I've never asked this, but how was the sex with your boyfriend?"

"Glenn was ..., good. Sex with him was fun, that was never our issue."

Liam is watching me.

"Were you always a top with him?" Rik continues.

"No, but mostly. Glenn fucked me a few times, but I never really enjoyed it. It was more of a "he's my boyfriend so I should let him fuck me when he really wants it" kind of thing."

"So romantic," Rik jokes. "People are going to be all over you in this town when they realize you're an actual top."

"Uh, why's that?"

"Most men around here tend to be bottoms. Even those who describe themselves as versatile want to be fucked. You'll see."

"Come look at how I'm binding Aiden's hands."

I get down on my knees behind Aiden and watch what Liam is doing.

"Looping it like this is better than tying because it is less likely to cut off circulation at his wrists. See this? "Liam tugs on the rope looped against itself around Aiden's wrists. "You should be able to get two fingers under the rope. That's how you know it's not too tight."

"Just like applying restraints on a patient."

"That's right," Rik says "Caine has more experience than he lets on."

I laugh. "Sure, but it's not sexy in the hospital."

"Ever?" Liam asks.

"Well, I mean …,"

Rik claps his hands. "Tell us your dirty nursing story."

"It's nothing like you're thinking. One time when I was floating to the emergency department, a patient was whacked out on meth and wouldn't let us draw blood. We opted for a urine test and two nurses pinned him down and held his hands over his head so that I could cath him for a urine sample. He was crazy muscular and his dick was hard the whole time; maybe being held down like that turned him on. So, sure, sometimes it's a little sexy, but not in a creepy way. Inserting a catheter is easier when the patient is errect, in case anyone is wondering"

"You better not shove anything up my dick," Aiden mumbles with a grin.

"That's actually a thing," Liam says. "Inserting metal or glass rods in the urethra. It's called sounding."

I frown. "Do you wear sterile gloves?"

Liam shakes his head.

"UTI , anyone?"

"Okay, get your head out of nursing mode." Liam points to Aiden's wrists. "A loop like this can't cinch tighter if he pulls on it. It also allows you to add space between the wrists when you're dealing with an ox like this."

Aiden struggles against the rope, flexing his muscles. It's very erotic.

"There's no way he can get out of this unless you secure the safety knot too close to his hands. Then he can untie himself."

"I see. Does that hurt your wrists?"

Aiden shakes his head. "It hurts my shoulders, but only a little. I suppose this is a good stretch."

"Maybe you'll finally be able to clean your own back."

I see him glaring at me in the mirror across the room.

Liam ruffles Aiden's hair. "Okay, the rest is up to you. Come meet us out at the pool when you boys have had your fun."

Rik rubs my back as he walks past me. "Take your time." Rik closes the door behind him.

"Think they locked us in here?"

Aiden shrugs.

"I actually expected them to stay in here and watch us."

He shifts his weight. "Naw, they're not like that."

"You guys never mess around?"

"We did in New Orleans. They both fucked me."

"What was that like?"

He chuckles. "You've had sex with Rik, so you know what he's like. Liam's ..., rougher, but in a fun way."

I tug on the black rope cutting into his sexy arms. "Are you comfortable like this?"

Aiden nods.

I assess his wrists. The loops Liam tied around his wrists are loose enough not to interrupt circulation. I need to master this knot. "Try to get out of this."

Aiden's shoulders and back flex as he pulls on the ropes.

I get up and stand in front of him. "I mean, really try."

I marvel at Aiden's incredible physique as he struggles to work his arms free from the rope. He works up a good sweat but doesn't come close to escaping.

He glares up at me. "Guess I'm your prisoner."

Fuck, I want to kiss him so bad. I have another idea, though, so I scan the gear hanging from the wall until I spot my target. I retrieve nipple clamps from the shelf and dangle them in front of me.

"What the fuck are you up to?"

"I'm just wondering," I say in an absolutely horrible German accent, "how much torture it will take to make you share your secrets."

"Ah Jesus, boy. I tell you everything."

"You tell me nothing!" I shout, still trying to sound like a German villain.

Aiden chuckles. "I can't take you seriously like this."

"Fine," I say in my normal voice. I fumble with the nipple clamps, which can be adjusted by turning a dial. I've seen them used in porn before, yet have never used them in real life. "Stand up."

He's clumsy with his hands roped behind his back like this, but he's able to stand. I walk him to the iron cross, as I've learned it is called, and turn him so that his back is against it. I locate the leather ankle restraints hanging on the wall and show them off as I walk back to him.

"You're enjoying yourself. "

I nod. Dropping to my knees, I fasten a restraint to his left ankle. He pulls his right foot away from me when I try to attach the other. "I'll take a paddle to your pretty ass if you fight me again."

"I wouldn't like that."

"That's why I'd do it."

He grunts.

"What?"

"You wouldn't do that. I know you too well."

I stand and look into his pale eyes. "You're right. But the longer you disobey me, the longer you have to go without dinner."

He laughs. "You son of a bitch."

I push his hair from his sweaty forehead. "I know your kryptonite."

"And I know yours."

"Oh?"

He nods. "You want to kiss me."

I lightly slap his face. "You are too cocky."

"But I'm right."

I pull away a bit, shaking my head. "Of course, I want to kiss you. I'm also looking forward to you cooking us dinner, so let's move things along." I fasten the other ankle restraint and tap the inside of his calves until he widens his stance. Using the carabiner clip attached to each restraint, I secure each ankle restraints to the metal rings on the iron cross near his feet. I get two more clips from a black metal bucket filled with them and clip the rope over his biceps to nearby rings. I pull on the iron cross, confirming it is well-secured to the bondage bed. I'm not sure if this immobilizes his upper body, but I think it will keep him from falling forward if he passes out or whatever.

Aiden has been watching me with intent this entire time. His hard cock is pointing up at the ceiling.

I pick up one of the nipple clamps and line it up with his left nipple. I turn the dial until it is tight enough to stay attached on its own. I turn it a little more until he hisses.

"Careful."

I turn it even more. "Where's the fun in that?"

I apply the other clamp, taking my time tightening it until he grunts. I tap the clamp with my finger a few times, watching his cock bounce with each tap.

"Damn, that hurts."

"But you love it."

He chuckles. "Sure, but that doesn't mean it doesn't hurt." His stomach rumbles, making us both laugh. "Ask your damn questions."

I stand back and appreciate what I have bound in front of me. "Fuck me, you're a beautiful man."

He smirks. "That's not a question, but thank you."

I'm not sure what I should ask him. He's highly aroused, and I'm afraid of ruining the moment. "What was it like, honestly, living on the streets in New Orleans?"

He looks at me a moment. "Scary."

"Elaborate, punk."

"Very scary."

He yelps when I move to tighten the nipple clamps. "Okay, geesh, just kidding. I was fifteen. I didn't have a cell phone or enough money for a bus to Baton Rouge, where my brothers still lived. I tried to stay out of sight because I feared my father would kill me if he found me. Hell, I don't know if he even tried to look for me."

"Have you talked to him since?"

Aiden shakes his head. "He could be dead for all I know."

"How did you survive, back then?"

"I tried my hand at pan-handling, but that went south. One night, some creepy old man offered me fifty dollars if I would follow him back to his hotel and let him blow me." He glares at me. "I was only fifteen."

"Fuck. What was that like?"

He shrugs. "I mean, he didn't hurt me or anything like that, but I felt so disgusting as he was blowing me, like I was the dirty one. I was pretty buff, even at that age, but he was so much stronger than me. I knew he could have done whatever he wanted to me in that moment, even though he was kind-of nice to me. I suppose that's what rape must feel like."

"Jesus."

"He offered me another hundred to spend the night with him. I would have done it for free just for the opportunity to sleep in a bed. He blew me again in the morning, bought me breakfast in the hotel lobby, and sent me on my way. I never saw him again. That's when I discovered my power over gay men."

"The amazing adventures of Muscle-Boy."

He smirks. "I don't know about amazing, but it really wasn't so bad after that first guy. I purchased weekly passes at a local gym so that I had a place to lift, shit and shower." I couldn't become a member without a driver licence or credit card, so the weekly passes were my only option. I worked out each morning, hung out near the rugby field at New Orleans City Park during the day, went back to the gym for a shower, then hung out near some of the gay bars."

"How ..., how did you meet clients."

He laughs at the word "clients". "Caine, it's just like you think of it as a business transaction. I suppose it was, though, because they paid me for a service. Anyway, I wore a tight t-shirt, leaned against a wall, and people would just walk up to me. My muscles made me look older and gay guys are ballsy as fuck. They have, like, no shame at all. Before I knew it, I was spending most nights in a random stranger's hotel room."

I keep poking his chest, watching his sunburned skin blanch. "And after all of that, you still consider yourself straight."

He chuckles, a sexy sound deep in his chest. "Is having sex with men the only qualifier for being gay? If you had sex with women, would that make you straight?"

"If I enjoyed having sex with women, and sought it out on a regular basis, I wouldn't call myself gay. Bi, maybe."

He shrugs. "You can call me bi if that helps you wrap your over-thinking mind around it, but I don't imagine falling in love with a man."

"But you could fall in love with a woman?"

"I mean, that sounds nice. I'm a little fucked in the head for an adult relationship, but I'm open to it."

I tighten one of the nipple clamps a bit, making him wince. "What the fuck, I'm answering your questions."

I run my fingers through his beard. "I can't help it. I love watching you squirm."

"I'm not kidding, you are totally Liam Junior."

"Does he do this to you?"

"Not at all. You should see how Liam treats their slave, though."

"You've watched them?"

"Few times. Liam and Rik treat me like a friend, but I don't want to push my luck by getting too close to them when they are in bondage master mode, you know?"

I nod. There's a question I've wanted to ask him since we met during Liam's birthday, but I'm worried I'm not going to like his response. "That night, in the hotel, when you were blindfolded and waiting for me."

"That was hot."

"Did Liam order you to do that?"

His face softens with recognition. "No way, man. Liam showed me your photo from SCRUFF and asked if I would be interested in doing that with you. You're sexy as fuck, so I was happy to do it."

"Oh."

"I don't think you get it. You're the first dude I've had sex with in years. I have sex with you because I love it, not because it's my duty."

"Sorry, I just assumed ..., I don't know."

"Caine, I'm not their sex slave. It's not that I wouldn't be, after all they've given me, but they don't treat me that way. I'm more like their adopted son. I mean, an adopted son who is inappropriately naked all the time, but I think they like seeing me naked."

I wrap my hand around his dick and squeeze until he hisses. "I mean, who wouldn't?"

"I'm just a big slab of meat to you."

"Exactly," I lie.

"Caine?"

"Hmm?"

"My arms are getting numb."

I sigh. I could stand here and enjoy this view all night.

"Any chance you're in the mood to release your slab of meat?"

I tug his beard. "All this talk of meat is making me hungry. Let's get you out of this gear so you can make us dinner."

Aiden smirks. "Yes, Sir."

I feel so comfortable here, sitting with Liam, Rik and Aiden in their library; so safe. These men not only allow me to be who I am, they encourage it. I prepared myself for admonishment when I admitted I hooked up with my married landlord, but Liam's only reply had been "of course." Liam has a way of looking at me rather than through me. I think my father has never done either and simply looks past me; around me.

"Where are you?" Liam asks from across the game table we encircle.

I look down at my glass of wine. "I'm going to miss you guys." My plan is to leave early tomorrow and make the six-hour drive to St. George, where I booked a motel for the night. I'll continue to Liam and Rik's Denver hotel the next day.

"You will come back," Rik states. "This is your home now."

Liam winks. "Your Denver contract ends in October. Take a few weeks off between contracts and come enjoy Leather Pride and Halloween. October is the best month to be here in the dessert."

I nod.

"You'll get into all kinds of trouble," Aiden adds from across the table.

"Yes," Rik agrees. "But there is plenty of trouble to be found in Denver."

"Speaking of which," Liam says, "I have an assignment for you. Two, actually."

"Should I take notes?"

Liam smiles. "No, cocky boy. But I do want you to send me a simple report of your observations at the hotel: how the staff handle various situations, how they treat the guests, and whatnot."

"I'm your spy."

"You're a twenty-six-year-old nurse booked in the penthouse suite for thirteen weeks: my staff will know you are important to us regardless of what you tell them. I'm sure they'll remain on their best behavior around you. Still, thirteen weeks gives you plenty of opportunity to see what's really going on in our hotel."

"We've never spent that much time at any of our properties," Rik adds. "We are excited to hear your observations."

I'm actually relieved they are asking me to do something because I have been feeling guilty about accepting their offer to stay in their hotel while I'm working in Denver. The fact they are putting me in their biggest suite is too much, but they continue to insist I am family and deserve the best.

"The second assignment," Liam states for the benefit of all of us, "is to practice your bondage. Your goal is to practice on at least one person each week."

"Yes," Rik says with excitement. "Create a personal add and announce to the world you are a big hung bondage daddy. They will line up for you."

Liam winks at me. "Maybe you'll even meet some gay guys this time."

"I can come visit," Aiden adds, "if, you know, you miss playing with a straight man."

I toss a cloth napkin at him. I allowed myself to fall for Aiden, against all of Liam's warnings. Leaving him will hurt, but I'm sure it's for the best. I need to figure myself out before I try understanding someone else. I remind myself, again, a relationship is the last thing I need at this point of my life. Maybe Liam was right about my needing to be liberated from my past and my shame. It's time to grow. It's time to accept who I am and start planning on who I want to be. It's time for new discoveries.

"Are you ready for your next adventure?" Liam asks as though reading my mind.

I am.

the end.

PREVIEW

Exclusive sneak peak of
"Mountain Bound: Caine's
Liberation Series Book Two".

The following is a scene from the upcoming book by Ren Stinnett, Mountain Bound: Caine's Liberation Series Book Two. Mountain Bound is scheduled for publication in March, 2024.

The hotel phone rings twenty minutes later and I am informed my guest will be escorted to the private elevator. I open the front door and wait in the entryway until the elevator door opens and Ben steps out with a big smile. He looks like his photos in the same manner I imagine most models look like their photos when you see them without makeup or perfect lighting: Real. He's wearing a plain white t-shirt, torn-up jeans, and red leather boots. His dark hair is spiked up high in a messy way, like he just got out of bed. His skin is pale and his tan eyes are glossy. He looks like a punk-rocker from the eighties. He also looks stoned. "You have a great smile, why don't you show it in any of your photos?"

"Ha, thanks." Ben follows me into my suite and removes a black and tan backpack I hadn't noticed and sets it on the floor of the entryway. "Holy shit," he says, looking around. "This place is crazy. How long are you staying here?"

"Another eleven weeks."

Ben spins around in the center of the main room as if taking it all in, then pokes his head into each of the rooms. There's something boyish in the way he walks around at such a fast pace, nearly skipping from room to room.

"Damn," he says as he returns to me. "You live in a palace."

"Right?"

He moves so close our chests nearly touch. He's a little taller and smells of smoke. He runs the back of his fingers up my left arm, causing a tingling sensation to rush to my dick. "May I have a kiss, your Royal Highness?"

I nod, taken by how deep and gravely his voice has become. He runs his fingers through my hair and cups my face in his large hands. I'm surprised by his gentle touch and the way he has somehow taken control of the situation as he lightly draws me toward his parted lips. He grazes his lips against mine. I am his at this moment.

He pulls an inch away but is still holding my face in his palms, his pale eyes looking at me as if searching for something. "Hi," he whispers.

"Wow," is all I can come up with as a response. "You're very intense."

He giggles. "I'm sorry, I'm a little high. Too much?"

I shake my head, nothing more. I continue looking up at his eyes, noticing his long eye-lashes and bushy dark eye brows. He has light stubble as though he shaved last night.

He kisses me again, even lighter than before. "Where's that shower?"

I take his hand and guide him to the main bedroom suite like I'm a child showing my father a new discovery, even though Ben is only eight years older than me. I bring him into the white marble bathroom with its black marble tub and countertops. The shower is so large it doesn't have doors: It's just a black-stoned cube the size of a small bedroom.

Ben whistles. "I would never leave this room. This bathroom is so big you could fit a bed in here. I would jack-off in this shower until my palms were bleeding."

"You can stay here as long as you like," I say before I can stop myself. I kiss him, catching Ben off-guard though he doesn't pull away. I draw back and stare at him, making him smile. "Damn, you're sexy."

He giggles again. "I appreciate that. I'm always nervous meeting guys online who don't know me from my bating sessions because my online photos are all modeling shots: They are me, yet … you know; not really me at all."

I nod. "You look better like this with your messy hair and natural eyebrows. You look more intense, more menacing in your photos."

"Hmm," is all he gives me.

I'm rubbing the small of his back just over his ass and realize I am clinging to him. I pull my hand away and try to be casual. "How long have you been modeling?"

Ben runs his fingers through his hair and sits on one of the large chairs by the tub. "Since I was twenty, so fourteen years now. It's never been a full-time gig, just something I do four or five times a year."

I've never met a professional model before. I'm shy and don't really like having my photo taken. "What's it like?"

Ben laughs. "Each session is completely different. Sometimes it's just a creepy old man taking pictures of me in his pool, and sometimes it's runway work. I'm tall and have a small waist, so designers like the way their clothes fall on me. I'm getting a little old for runway work but I have a session in Bali two months from now which I'm looking forward to: it only pays two grand for a week but they are flying my there in business class and I get to stay in this massive house up in the rice paddies of Ubud near a monkey forest. I've never been there before. Have you?"

All I want is to strip him down and drag him into the shower. Instead, I sit in the other chair. "Nope. I've never left the country. How did you get into modeling?"

"I just fell into it. I used to post bate videos way before bating sites came out. Someone watched one and said I should model. I thought he was hitting on me but he was very professional. I was amazed at the way he could make me look through his lens. Before I knew what was happening, I was being paid to let people take my picture."

"Tell me about your bating sessions."

Ben shifts his weight. "Like modeling, I just kind of fell into it. I've always loved jacking off—"

"Who doesn't?"

"No," Ben continues. "I mean, I really love it. Sure, everyone masturbates but most guys do it as a means to an end. Most guys are satisfied cranking one out in a few minutes in a bathroom stall or all over a potted plant."

"A plant?"

Ben nods. "Don't ask. Anyway, I think most guys rush it just to relieve tension because they are ashamed to pleasure themselves; they are ashamed of their body and how it works."

His mentioning shame makes me think of Liam.

"I think I've taken my masturbation to a level of artistry in which my entire body becomes my source of pleasure. It's not about an orgasm and I will often go weeks without cumming."

"Jesus, I can't go a day."

"You can," Ben says with a laugh. "You just don't want to. For me, it's about bringing myself to the highest possible peak of ecstasy and keeping myself there until my entire body is vibrating with sexual energy. It is so much better than sex, which is why I consider myself a solosexual."

"You ... only have sex alone?" I fumble.

"Uh, not always alone. I guess it means different things

to different people, but for me solosexual means I prefer masturbation over traditional sex. I mean, I've had normal sex but I don't really enjoy it because it is often all about the other person. I'd rather just focus on myself."

"Selfish."

Ben smiles. "Totally selfish. Well, I masturbate in front of thousands of others via bate video sites; so maybe I'm not all that selfish."

"People pay to watch you masturbate."

"Yes. They pay a lot, believe it or not. It can get weird with complete strangers tipping you and I don't love the idea of them telling me what to do, such as 'show me your hole' or 'say my name as you shoot' just because they are giving me money. But I'm a true exhibitionist: I love being watched, showing off. I love the idea that people get aroused by watching me arouse myself. Does that make sense?"

It wouldn't have before meeting Aiden, but now I just nod.

"Money is relative and jacking off on camera isn't going to make me rich, but I make enough to pay my bills."

"Do you have a normal job? I mean no offense but ..., you know what I mean."

"I don't, aside from the occasional modeling gig."

I must have made an odd expression because Ben starts laughing. "What's your sign?"

"Pices, why?"

"Hmm. When's your birthday?"

"Need the last four of my social as well?"

"Yes, and then we need to discuss the details of your car's warranty."

"February twenty-ninth."

"Seriously?

I nod.

"Well, that explains everything."

"Does it?"

He laughs. He has one of those great laughs, open and unrestrained. "I'm kidding, but it's fun to make you look uncomfortable like this." He stands. "I know we agreed to you roping me to the bed and jacking me off, Leap Year, but how about I show you how to really masturbate?"

I nod, watching him step out of the bathroom. Ben returns a few seconds later with his backpack.

"Some people like jacking off dry, but I prefer using lubricant and brought some with me."

"I have lube," I say but Ben motions me to stop when I begin rising from the chair. He removes a white and blue tub from his backpack.

"I only use Alboline."

I shrug. "Never heard of it."

He hands me the container. "It's actually make-up remover, but it is the best lube for jacking off. It's super slippery, won't dry out so it lasts forever, doesn't have any weird scent and wipes off clean. It's basically solidified mineral oil so it will stain sheets, but I rarely jack-off in bed so that's not an issue for me." Ben pulls his t-shirt over his head and tosses it on the floor. The tattoo on the left side of his neck goes all the way down to his clavicle and stretches out to the top of his shoulder. "Just talking about it makes me horny," Ben continues. "May we take that shower you promised, Your Highness?"

He is removing his boots before I can nod, then struggles a bit to pull his tight pants off. He's not wearing underwear and his dick is plumped up in a semi-erection. His pubic hair is trimmed short but he has nice furry legs. He steps into the shower and studies the various knobs and buttons before turning to me with a goofy grin. "This looks complicated."

I strip down to my black boxer-briefs and join him. I

activate the large square shower head in the middle of the marbles ceiling which gives the effect of a warm rain, then show him how he can adjust the lighting and how all the various shower heads and steam spouts work. "The shower is big enough that you can stand here fully dressed without getting wet, except when you turn on the steam vents. I don't recommend turning those on until you are happy with the temperature."

Ben nods and begins fiddling with the controls. He changes the shower lights to deep red, one of dozens of color options. I step out of the shower and turn the bathroom lights off. There are no windows in the bathroom so the only light is the red glow of the shower.

I remove my underwear, suddenly feeling shy in front of Ben. Grabbing his tub of Alboline, I step into the shower which is hotter than I would have selected. I set the lubricant on one of the two large benches on either side of the shower and rub Ben's stubbled chest.

"I know," he says as if answering a question. "The stubble is weird but I had a photo shoot last week for a swimwear company and they shaved me. I had to fight to keep them from shaving my legs." Ben glances at an inset shelf where I keep my razor and shaving gel. "You can shave it if the stubble bothers you."

I nod. The stubble doesn't bother me at all but the idea of shaving his chest makes my dick thicken. I reach for the shaving gel but Ben grabs my arm to stop me.

"The Albolene works better, and feels better. I'm assuming it's better for your skin than that chemical gel you have there, but what do I know? You're the nurse."

My look must display surprise because it makes him smile.

"You included your social media link in your profile. Did you really think I wouldn't check you out before agreeing to come over and let you take control of me?" Ben opens the Albolene and rubs some on his chest and belly, continuing down until his dick glistens in the red light of the shower. I love how casual he is, rubbing the stuff into his skin like he is applying suntan lotion rather than attempting to look sexy. He begins stroking his dick with his left hand.

"You seem to be the one in control here," I say while reaching for the razer. I massage his chest to evenly distribute the cream and then hold the razer at the top of his sternum. "Hold still. I don't want to cut you."

"My next photoshoot isn't for a month, so do your worst."

I wrap my arm around him so that my hand is on his back to steady me as I draw the razer across his chest. Ben continues his slow stroking in silence while watching me. I take my time, being careful. I've shaved my ex-boyfriend's chest several times but Glenn had a peach fuzz of chest hair compared to Ben. I imagine how sexy he must look with his chest untrimmed and am reminded of Mitch, my landlord from Palm Springs, and his beautifully hairy chest. I tend to be attracted to smooth chests but I'm learning to appreciate the raw manliness of body hair.

It takes a while to finish shaving his chest and belly and when I am finished, I step back to admire my work. He is shiny with Albolene and glowing red in the steamy shower. Still stroking his dick to a slow unheard rhythm, Ben stands under the showerhead and rinses off. I move behind him and wrap my arms around his waist and avoid the urgency to press my dick against his hard butt, being careful to respect his boundaries. I rub my hands up and down his smooth torso.

"Does that feel better?" he whispers.

"You feel great."

Ben pulls away from me and sits on one of the benches. He lifts one foot onto the bench and returns to masturbating, drawing his hand up and down his thick shaft at an incredibly slow rate. His has a nice dick, probably a little smaller than mine but it looks huge against to his tiny waist.

"Now I understand why people pay to watch you jack off."

Ben giggles and slides over, patting his right hand on the

bench. "Come join me, Leap Year. Let me show you how I like to do it."

I sit next to him and realize the marble bench is warmed, something I've never noticed before. Ben reaches across his body and dips his right hand into his tub of make-up cream, then wraps his hand around my dick. I hiss at the contact and wish I had jacked-off this morning because I don't know how long I can last with him touching me like this.

"Take your mind away from your dick," Ben says, nearly purring. "Include your whole body in your masturbation session."

I lick his shoulder, inhaling deep as though able to draw him in. "What do you mean?"

"Your dick is only one part of your sensual being." Ben speaks like he strokes: soft, deep and deliberate. He leans over and twists so that his mouth is over my chest.

"You're very limber."

"Yoga," he responds. "Our body is loaded with erogenous zones, such as your nipples," he licks my left nipple, which makes my eyes roll back. He kisses my neck and runs his tongue up my Adam's apple. "Your neck. Your armpits. Your ass. The secret to better masturbation is to stop making your dick your focal point."

I hear what he's saying but can't stop staring at his hand around my dick.

Ben releases his grip when I begin panting. "Relax. Breathe." He turns a bit so that he is facing me. "Let me show you."

Ben puts on a show for me, rubbing his chest and abs, fingering his ass, and licking his tight biceps. I'm fascinated. I try imitating him but I am not limber enough for some of his tricks. I'm so aroused I'm afraid to even touch my dick, so I focus on Ben and the way he bites his lower lip as though in agony. Hours pass in this steamy red shower and I realize at this moment, with Ben sitting across from me like this, I can sit with him like this and watch him all day.

Another hour of watching him stroke his dick passes. I

don't know how he does it. He must recognize my frustration because he leans forward and begins rubbing my dick.

"Careful," I whisper. "I'm so close it hurts."

"You're doing great," his grip intensifies, making me moan. His rhythm changes enough to keep me from shooting. "You want to cum. You deserve to cum."

I sit on my hands and fight the urge to grab him as he continues teasing me. He brings me so close to cumming I want to scream before he changes his grip just enough to keep me from crossing the threshold. My knees begin to tremble.

"Okay," he says. "Show me what you've got."

His touch drives me insane and I hold my breath as my pulse deafens me. Ben is kissing my eyes, my face, and my neck. I howl as I begin to cum—savage and unrestrained—and find myself sobbing by the end. Ben continues kissing my face, stroking my hair.

I finally open my eyes, in love with him in this moment as my entire body thrums with sexual energy. "Holy fuck," I growl. "I've never shot so hard before."

Ben winks. "I told you. That was only a few hours: imagine the energy released if we did this all weekend."

"That would kill me."

"Ha, you just need to work up to it." Ben stand, stretches, and returns under the shower head. His dick is still hard.

"Are you going to get off?"

He shakes his head. "Naw, I'm just getting started. I love the feeling of being this horny."

We clean each other until we are both covered in lather, then I turn on multiple shower heads so we are rinsed from every angle. My arm is around his waist and I can't bring myself to break our connection until he finally pulls away and glances around the bathroom. "I'm not wearing my glasses," he says with a smile. "What time is it."

I step out of the shower with reluctance and look at the clock over the sinks. We were in that shower nearly four hours. "It's five."

"No wonder I'm so hungry,"

I nod. "Want to grab dinner."

Ben steps out of the shower and wraps one of the huge towels over his shoulders. "I'd love to, but I'm on a crazy diet for the upcoming photoshoot and I'm working tonight."

"Send me the link, maybe I'll spend the night watching you."

"Naw, I'd rather you be my bate-buddy rather than a client. Let's do this again, cool?"

I nod. It's more than cool because I love the idea of seeing him again.

Ben pulls his pants on. "Are you really staying in this big place alone?"

"I am. Why?"

Ben steps forward and kisses my forehead. "Just refreshing. People usually lie to me."

"Hmm. You have my number, so call anytime you miss the shower."

"Ha, then I'll be calling every day."

How terrible, I think with a smirk. I'm so proud of myself for refraining from saying it out loud.

REN STINNETT

ABOUT THE AUTHOR

Ren Stinnett

Ren Stinnett was introduced to the fetish community in his thirties and has been writing about his adventures and observations for years. Several of his stories were featured in various gay publications but it wasn't until 2023, with the full support and encouragement of his family, that he decided to publish in book format.

When he's not writing, you can find him curled up with a juicy book, roping a sexy man in a variety of compromising positions, looking for new adventures, or spending time with his amazingly non-judgmental family.

Made in the USA
Las Vegas, NV
29 January 2024